Freyja and the Brisingamen Necklace

By

J. C. Enno

Illustrations by Liz McKenzie

For Sam, Joseph and Caitlin.

My dancing fireflies.

CONTENTS

1	Light the Path	1
2	Old Man Folke	15
3	Compass	25
4	The Protector	35
5	Water Blossom Pea Tree	45
6	The Worthy	57
7	Reward	69
8	Gypsies of Asgard	79
9	Mountain Puzzle	91
10	Dwarf Brothers Three	103
11	The First Task	115
12	The Second Task	127
13	The Final Task	139
14	Holding Hope	151
15	Unfulfilled Wishes	161
16	Star and Sun	173
17	The Brisingamen Necklace	183
	Epilogue	193

Chapter 1

Light the Path

Freyja stood hesitantly before the closed bedroom door. Timid and fearful ever since she was a child, it was her twin brother who was the brave one. He always took the first step and shielded her from harm.

When Freyja was born, she could have been mistaken for any other babe. She screamed upon entering the world and cried to communicate her needs. Whether it was a hungry belly wanting food, demanding a clean nappy, or the desire for sleep against her mother's chest, Freyja could rival any other newborn in the screaming arena.

As she grew, you would have thought nothing unusual. She learned to crawl before walking, placed every object in her mouth regardless if it was edible, and absorbed her surroundings with a curiosity that only comes from the distinctly young. Yes, nothing indicated that Freyja was anything but an ordinary child beloved by her parents.

However, when you were a child of Asgard, ordinary was never enough.

Freyja stared at her feet. The woollen socks kept the cold from the floorboards seeping into her bones. Her head leaned against her brother's bedroom door, and she closed her eyes. Before walking in, she promised herself she wouldn't cry, but memories of a happier time caused a well of emotion to overflow.

*   *   *

The memory unfolded from the guarded confines of her heart.

Freyja stared at her feet; they were bare and she was running.

"Little sister, you really need to learn to keep up," shouted Frey. The forest danced with light and shadow as the setting sun's rays cascaded through the treetops, and a cool breeze caused branches and leaves to sway and ripple.

Freyja didn't know why they were rushing. There was plenty of time before sunset, and the fairy folk would not begin the conjuring until darkness was upon them. The mossy ground was soft and bouncy, and Freyja watched as her brother raced ahead like a rabbit that was born to bound.

"Why is everything a race to you?" she called out, her chest heaving. Frey flitted in and out of her vision; his form obscured by trees and shadows, only to reappear a moment later, his chestnut hair catching the sunlight.

"Why walk when we can run?" he answered, his laughter ringing in the air and his dagger held skyward like a torch. "We are warriors. When Lord Odin orders a call to arms, all men and women will rush to defend Asgard!"

This was not strictly true. Their peaceful village housed bakers, poets, dressmakers, craftsmen, and boat makers. Yes, they were all taught to fight, but that didn't mean all Asgardians were passionate about wielding a sword. Freyja would have pointed this out, but her brother was too far ahead.

Leaping cautiously over a gully, she crawled up the embankment to discover Frey standing before a lake. Though they were both fourteen summers old, he was a head taller than her.

The waters spread out before them, strangely still like a silver mirror reflecting the skies. They had arrived at the home of the fairy folk. Freyja placed her hands on her knees as she exhaled hot steam into the cold evening.

"Something's not right," said Frey.

"Yes, I'm exhausted. You'll have to carry me on your back when we go home," said Freyja, her eyes glued to the ground.

"Be quiet."

Freyja looked to the sun, which was still descending behind the horizon and signalled that they hadn't missed the conjuring. It also meant that with dusk upon them, the fairies should have emerged. Like a thousand fireflies, they would float out of the lake and begin the summoning of the water elementals. The ceremony that followed was a dazzling display of fire and water that bewitched Freyja every time.

But tonight, nothing moved. The surface of the lake looked hard and impenetrable. The stillness felt oppressive as Freyja stood close behind her brother.

"The fairies should be gathering." The words came out strained, like she was inhaling something thick and sticky. She coughed. "I want to leave."

Frey raised a hand for silence. He looked over to the far side of the lake and pointed. Amongst the tall grass, Freyja glimpsed movement. Smooth and fluid, the creature slithered along the edges of the lake.

"Scorhyde," said Frey. "It's hunting. The fairies are trying to hide."

Freyja could see the serpentine creature; its tapered wings were folded in on itself and two curled horns protruded from its head. In the dim light, she guessed it was twice as long as she was tall. She tugged at her brother's arm. "That thing is

4

poisonous, and flies faster than an Asgardian arrow. We must flee," she said.

"The fairy folk will not be able to hide much longer. Even underwater, their magic will start to glow, and then it will be over," explained Frey. "The scorhyde can move as easily in water as it does in air. We cannot abandon them."

Freyja could see her brother's calm breathing; he was poised for action, while her panic began to rise like the tide. The scorhyde opened its mouth and let out a fine mist. She knew this was the thick substance that permeated the air. The creature used it to trap its prey. Any fairy that sought to escape would have its wings weighed down by the sticky cloud that hovered over the lake.

It was now dark, and Freyja wanted the earth to swallow her so she could hide from the ghastly monster. She was about to attempt one final plea to her brother when the unmistakable glow of a fairy appeared near the middle of the lake.

Without hesitation, the scorhyde shot straight at the light.

"Begone!" shouted Frey.

The scorhyde halted mid-flight and stared with obsidian eyes at him. Annoyed by the intrusion, the creature let out a horrible hiss that unleashed Freyja's panic.

"Run!" she shouted.

The scorhyde opened its leathery wings and flew at Frey, fangs spread wide aiming for his face. Freyja screamed as the creature sought to swallow her brother's head whole. Frey stood knees bent, and with one smooth motion, he pulled out his dagger and thrust upward in front of his face. With violent accuracy, the blade went up through the base of the scorhyde's mouth and through the top of its head.

The creature thrashed wildly, but Frey brought his dagger down in a wide arc and nailed the scorhyde's head into the ground. Its thick tail swung and almost swept Freyja off her feet, if not for her brother lifting her into his arms and jumping out of the way. It was all over in seconds.

Freyja whimpered as her brother held her close.

"Running for joy and running for fear are not the same thing little sister," he said with a wry smile. The fairy folk rose from the lake like tiny fire lit lanterns floating through the air and surrounding the pair in thanks.

Freyja couldn't bring herself to be angry at her brother. "After the conjuring, I get to ride on your back all the way home."

*   *   *

Freyja wiped her eyes. The memory folded back into the treasure box of her heart as she stamped her socked feet to keep warm. "No more crying," she reprimanded herself.

However, upon seeing her twin brother, pale and weak, a sob rose in her throat. This was not the strong, courageous Frey that was her shield, confidant, and best friend. Her brother would have woken up hours ago, snuck into the kitchen, climbed the highest shelf, and stolen biscuits from the cookie jar for the two of them to eat.

It had to be someone else, she thought. Shuffling on padded feet, Freyja approached clasping her hands. The only sounds came from the moans and wheezing breath of the frail figure whose eyes were closed in feverish sleep.

With the arrival of the white frost in Asgard, a sudden illness came upon the village, and many children were struck down. Einar was the first, collapsing in a heap while tending the fields. Then brothers Birger and Brant, sons of Calder the miller, succumbed while repairing the windmill. When little Eerika did not wake the next morning, her forehead clammy, bedsheets soaked from sweat, and her whispered words issued forth from nightmares, the villagers knew an epidemic was on their hands.

After consulting with old man Folke, who visited each child and referred to his ancient scrolls, he concluded the disease was the rare tetanarium. An illness not seen in decades that attacked only Asgardian youth through the smallest of wounds.

"All the sick children have some sort of cut or abrasion," rumbled Folke. "The cure is a special stone called the brisingr, buried in the ice capped mountains to the north. When ground into powder, dissolved in liquid, and ingested, it will fight the disease."

The problem was the northern mountains were guarded by Skadi the Jotunn, a female frost giant renowned for her hatred toward the Asgard people.

The moment the village elders asked for volunteers to journey north, it was Freyja's father, Njord, and her brother who raised their hands proclaiming that they would seek out the brisingr stone. Freyja had stood hiding behind her mother, Nerthus, and watched in awe as Frey did not hesitate. He had displayed a courage that she could never find, but on the morning of their departure, she found her brother collapsed in his bedroom.

"It was a couple of days ago," he said through bated breath as she rushed to his side. "A mere scratch from working the furnace with Blacksmith Gudbrand. I thought nothing of it." These were the last words before the fever overtook him, and a fear gripped her heart like a vice.

With an urgency to save not only the children, but also his own son, Njord journeyed forth that morning determined to bring back a brisingr stone.

Meanwhile, Freyja waited. Each day she stood before her brother's bedroom door, frozen in fear. She would use every ounce of her strength to enter, and hold back tears at the sight of Frey wilting like a sun-starved flower. Sitting by his bed, reading him stories, and staring out the window, she hoped to see her father appear over the rise of the hill that led down to their village with a triumphant smile. And each day the sun would set with her hopes unfulfilled.

By the ninth day, Freyja felt her heart diminishing. The pain of her brother's deterioration, and the growing fear of her father's continued absence, caused her heart to shrink into some deep, dark place. A place where it could avoid being pierced by the ominous dread that hung in the air and flooded her insides.

By the tenth day, she feared the worst: that her father was lost in the frozen mountainous wasteland, or Skadi had slain him. The hope within

9

Freyja began fluttering like a tiny flame trying to resist the wind. When dusk arrived on that tenth day and still no sign of her father, Freyja leaned over her twin brother's pallid face, and felt utterly helpless.

"It should have been me that was struck by this disease," she whispered, choking on her tears. "You would have gone with father and protected each other. You would be back by now with the brisingr stone and cured us all."

The tears ran down her face, sparkling like drops of amber from the rays of the setting sun. Tiny jewels carrying the despair of all that she felt. "I'm lost Frey," she whimpered. "Tell me what to do." The plea mixed with her teardrops and tasted bitter. She rested her head against the side of her brother's face.

It was dark by the time Freyja's sobbing stopped. She had dozed off in dreamless slumber, and awoke rubbing her eyes at the stars glistening in the night sky. With all the emotion released, she felt drained, but it was a welcome feeling that brought a sense of clarity.

Staring at the moons, Asmund and Asta, suspended in the Asgardian night, a calmness ran through her body down to the tips of her toes. Asta, the smaller white moon, was almost in line with

Asmund, the larger yellow moon. The two celestial bodies moved in opposite directions, and once a year would meet up together with Asta in front and Asmund behind like a halo. It was a stunning event that inspired many an Asgardian poet. Frey always took her up to the hill on the night the moons would join. The thought caused the darkness inside her to subside a little. She turned and tucked the blankets around her brother.

As she kissed him on the cheek, she said, "I think I know what to do Frey. Thank you." For the first time in her life, a purpose formed in a clear and direct way. "I'm going to save you and *I* will take *you* up the hill to see Asta and Asmund become one." With those promised words, she closed the bedroom door and went to retrieve her lantern and cloak from the cupboard.

Walking downstairs, the rhythmic sounds of creaking came floating through the air from the sitting room. With all her tears already shed, Freyja felt only a dull ache as she entered to see her mother in a rocking chair staring out the window.

"Mama, it's cold in here. Why haven't you lit the fireplace?" Freyja tried to act normal, but the question came out shrill. She busied herself with placing fresh blocks of wood and tinder, and a welcome blaze filled the room with warmth.

Nerthus continued to rock back and forth, mumbling words spoken like a mantra that Freyja could not understand. She was a portly woman, with thick ropes of blonde hair, a silver ring through the helix of her left ear, kind eyes that were the same as Freyja's, and rosy cheeks when she was excited or happy. Those cheeks were now sallow and without mirth. Her mother appeared oblivious to her presence until she placed a quilt on her legs.

"Freyja?" Her eyes came into focus away from the window, away from some distant place that Freyja could not reach.

"Yes mama, it's me," she whispered.

Nerthus gripped her arms in a gentle but firm way. "I cannot see your father. I see naught but shadows."

Freyja suppressed the feeling of dread. The strength and graceful features of her mother were still there buried under those swollen eyes, and dishevelled hair. Nerthus could match the ferocity of the Valkyries. Freyja had seen her spar against her father, and her skill with sword and shield matched anyone in the village. She knew her mother would throw herself into the maws of the great wolf, Fenrir, to defend those she loved. But against a foe that was unseen, a disease that you could not swing a blade at, she had dwindled into despair.

Freyja watched as her mother spent the days caring for her sick brother, and then planting herself like a forlorn flower in the evening, swaying back and forth in her rocking chair, waiting for Njord to return. Her routine was reduced to these two tasks. It was clear that Nerthus's strength stemmed from her family, but with her husband gone and her son falling further into darkness, the dire situation had overwhelmed her.

"You need to rest mama," said Freyja, kissing her on the forehead.

Her daughter's permission appeared to release her. Nerthus let out a long sigh as if by staying awake, the hope inside her would not be extinguished, but through Freyja's words she was allowed a moment of respite. Freyja felt strange that the roles were reversed as she watched her mother close her eyes.

When she was sure her mother was asleep, Freyja departed. Her lantern held aloft, a floating light in the darkness. Walking briskly along the stony path, there was only one place she could think of to start. She went to see old man Folke.

Chapter 2

Old Man Folke

Old man Folke was a giant, grizzly of a man whose beard was the colour of rich earth, and reached past his waist. With a bulbous nose that stuck out almost as far as his gigantic paunch, if he lay down he could have been mistaken for a congregation of small mounds. His squinty eyes were like two tiny inkwells, but looked too large for his face whenever he wore his square rimmed glasses. The thick lenses magnified his eyes to ridiculous proportions. His arms and hands looked capable of crushing boulders, and his large feet made deep impressions wherever he walked. Freyja swore he was like a moving tree with heavy roots, which he lumbered to pull up and then replant with every step.

You would never have guessed his mind was as sharp as the fangs of the world serpent, Jormungandr. He looked more suited to be a lumber jack, or working in one of the palace kitchens in Asgard given his enormous palate for food and wine. In reality, his knowledge of ailments and medicines rivalled Asgard's great libraries.

To Freyja, he petrified her. There was no doubt that if he wanted to, he could snap her delicate frame like a twig. But on this night, fear was put aside as she raced to the lone hut that rested at the base of the hill. A chill wind rippled through her long auburn hair, causing her to lift the hood of her cloak to give some protection.

When she arrived, the smells of pork roasting on a spit wafted up through the chimney of Folke's stone hut. A nearby gully could be heard behind the house. Its trickling water running over mossy stones signalled the border of the forest where Folke often foraged for herbs, mushrooms and wild flowers for his strange concoctions.

Out of breath, she stood on the top stone step before a giant redwood door, and gathered her thoughts.

"I should have brought a bag of tinkleberries," she whispered to the door. The golden syrupy fruit would appeal to Folke's sweet tooth, and put him in a good mood. Berating herself for the missed opportunity, she raised an unsteady hand and knocked lightly. Part of her hoped Folke wouldn't hear the knock. It was the part that wanted to shrink back into its shell and run back home.

"Come in! The door's open!" boomed a voice that caused Freyja to jump out of her skin.

She turned the handle and was surprised at how easily the heavy door swung open. Its well-oiled hinges didn't even creak as light streamed out from within. Turning off her lantern, Freyja blinked at the brightness as she stepped over the threshold. A cheery fire was burning from a large brazier by the door. While her brother had visited Folke on occasion, this was Freyja's first time seeing the inside of the old man's home. The sight that greeted her could only be described as a jungle.

Leafy potted plants sat on the floor, and hung off chains from the ceiling. Orchids the size of Freyja's arm wrapped around bamboo stalks that shot up from long earthen troughs filled with rich soil. Vines with pink, purple and yellow flowers wound their way along beams and down posts that held up the roof. Grapes and berries sagged in bunches from nets that were strung up to form canopies.

Freyja wondered how all these plants grew indoors, and received the answer when she spied moonbeams streaming through glass windows that formed part of the wooden roof. Squeezing past a redwood bench that held jars of pickled vegetables, and dried peppers and garlic bulbs that dangled from hooks, she saw the large back of Folke, kneeling down, hunched over a bunch of pots.

"Hello Folke. It's me, Freyja."

"Freyja?" said Folke. "My wee child, what brings you to my humble home?"

"I need to talk to you," she replied, shy as a mouse. Freyja approached wondering what the old man was doing.

"Come closer then." He waved her over. "Cast your eyes on these little beauties." Folke was busy transferring various green plants into new pots.

"Are these for your medicines?" she asked.

"Ho ho! Not these little wonders. You wouldn't want to waste these on bitter medicines," he chuckled. "I bought them off a merchant who returned from Midgard. I've no idea how he procured passage across the Bifrost, but somehow he managed to bring back these herbs." Freyja had heard of Midgard from her father, the human world connected to Asgard by the rainbow bridge, Bifrost. Very rarely was any Asgardian permitted to journey to Midgard.

Folke pointed to each plant like a child choosing sweets. "That's mint, that one's rosemary, coriander, basil, lemongrass, parsley and thyme."

Freyja stared at the strange plants. "You use them in cooking?"

He nodded in such an animated fashion, it caused his beard to shake. "Combined with the herbs we grow on Asgard, I can discover culinary delights you would have never dreamed of before!"

Freyja gave silent thanks to the tiny leafed plants, for Folke was in a jovial mood. To get his help would require treading in the right places. "That's wonderful," she said, feigning interest.

Much to her dismay, Folke sensed her disingenuous tone. Placing a basil bush delicately into a clay pot, he swivelled on giant feet, and peered at her. With one large hand, he retrieved his glasses from a pocket, and placed them on his bulbous nose. His eyes enlarging in a way that froze tiny Freyja where she stood. As if understanding for the first time the significance of her presence at this late hour, he asked, "Does Nerthus know you are here?"

Under that penetrating gaze, poor Freyja could not manage even a shake of her head. Her mouth went dry, and the muscles in her neck stiffened. She wanted to flee but couldn't even lift a finger. Her silence did little to appease Folke's growing suspicion. As he rose like an oak tree bursting from the earth, the moonbeams reflected off his glasses warning that further refusing to answer would be foolish. "Do not make me repeat myself lass."

Her heart thumped against her chest as Freyja answered, "Mother doesn't know… my brother… Frey…"

"Yes, the tetanarium," he said. "I've done all I can child. It's up to your father now. The brisingr stone is the only hope."

"Father hasn't returned," she said.

"What do you want me to do?" he asked, anger rising. "I am not a warrior. You should be speaking to the elders if you want to send someone after your father."

"But…"

"But nothing!" shouted Folke. "If the brisingr is not brought to me, I cannot make the potion required. Your brother and the rest of the infected children will die."

The finality of the statement caused Freyja to crumble to her knees as tears began to stream down her face.

"Oh! By Odin's beard!" said Folke, running a palm down his face in frustration. "This is why I never had children." He bent down and picked Freyja roughly up by the shoulders. "Stand on your feet child! What would your brother think if he saw you blubbering away like this?"

The question brought Freyja back to her senses. Her sobbing calmed as she took several deep breaths. Craning her neck, she could see Asmund and Asta in the night sky through the glass ceiling. It would only be a couple of more weeks before they would become one. There was no time to waste.

"There must be something else that can be done," she said, surprised by the firmness of her own voice.

Folke raised an eyebrow at Freyja's sudden composure. "There is nothing else. The brisingr is the key."

"Is there nowhere else where it can be found?"

With barely held restraint, Folke removed his glasses, and pinched the bridge of his nose with one hand. "As I told the elders, the northern mountains are the only place they have been discovered. I gave your father specific instructions to the cave where Skadi lives. She hoards her treasures there. As dangerous as it might be, it is the most likely place where brisingr stones can be found."

"Inside her cave?" asked Freyja as a curious expression passed over her face.

"Do your ears not work lass? It is bad enough I have to repeat what I have already explained to the elders." He stomped over to his redwood bench, and pulled a pickle from one of the jars. Popping it into his mouth brought back some of his patience as he savoured the taste. "Like any precious gem, you're not going to stumble upon them by the side of the road. Brisingr stones are rare, and buried in those frigid mountains."

"You would have to dig for them," whispered Freyja more to herself than to Folke.

"Of course, you dig for them," replied Folke exasperated.

"Dwarves," she said.

"What?"

"The dwarves mine those mountains. Wouldn't they have found brisingr stones?"

Folke paused before popping a second pickle into his mouth. "There are mines," he said, stroking his beard. "They're abandoned though. It's possible even the remnants of the brisingr could be useful. All that digging, some of the brisingr stones were broken into dust, but it wouldn't be enough to cure all the children who are ill. A single stone is what we need, but the dwarves dug most of it out and then left. They could've gone on but they wanted to steer clear of Skadi's cave." He chewed a third pickle thoughtfully. "There might be a small group that stayed behind, still chipping away, but if Skadi ever found them they'd be her next dinner."

"So, there might still be some dwarves there?"

"They are shifty, greedy little creatures who would dig to the bottom of Asgard to find gemstones, so who knows? Maybe. The problem is even if you found one, and they happened to have a brisingr stone, they wouldn't simply hand it over to you because you asked nicely. They would demand something ten times the price before parting with the stone. You would have a better chance with Skadi." He looked up at the moons. "Now enough with these questions. You have overstayed your welcome child. I do not want your mother discovering your bed empty. Remove these thoughts from your head and go home."

Freyja departed and clutched her cloak around her chest. Leaving the warmth of Folke's home, she felt gooseflesh cover her body as chill winds blew, and snowflakes arrived to cover the village. Turning over the conversation in her mind, Folke had made it clear that there was little chance of finding dwarves in the mountains. As she sought to return home, head bent down against winter's breath, Freyja held on to a tiny part of her heart that disagreed. A tiny part that held onto the hope that even if it was just a little chance, it was still a chance.

Chapter 3

Compass

In the light of the next day, Freyja awoke to the sight of the village covered in a pristine blanket of snow. Normally the children would already be out making forts. Their laughter and shouts filling the air as they waged war on each other with snowballs, and the ground dotted with their little footprints.

However, on this particular morning the village was silent. Nature was untouched, a blank canvas of white as if time stopped, and everything was frozen in its place. There were no children running outside or sliding down the big hill on wooden sleds. There was no movement anywhere except for the windmill near the west river. Its blades rotated stiffly against the cold.

All the children were being kept indoors. The threat of the tetanarium meant every parent dare not risk their child playing in the snow. The slightest cut or scrape from a snowball fight, or falling off a sled, or slipping on ice could expose them to the disease. Freyja stared at the top of the hill, willing for her father's return but to no avail.

Her venture to old man Folke produced a tiny ray of hope, and she spent most of the night planning her next steps. A scroll slid off her blanket and fell onto the floor as she shifted in bed. The scroll unrolled to reveal a map of her village and the nearby surroundings. She had stared at it all night until her eyelids became heavy from fatigue.

Growing up, she never went outside her village without Frey. It was he who had the adventurer's spirit and infused her with an enthusiasm that squashed her fears of exploring new places. So long as her brother was there, she never felt afraid. Together they discovered what lay beyond the hill and recorded their findings on their worn piece of parchment. It proved to be time well spent as she contemplated her journey north.

From under her pillow, she pulled out a round, flat object that fit in her hand. It was a compass that her father had given her, but it wasn't any old compass. This compass was infused with Asgardian magic. Freyja could see four dials within its face, each dial with its own coloured arrow. The symbols for north, south, east and west representing the compass rose were etched in each dial. On the edge of the device were four crowns, which could be pushed or spun.

Now a normal compass always points north, but Freyja's could be controlled by setting each dial to a specific place. Its corresponding arrow would always guide her back to that location. Her father had set one of the dials to always point to their village, so even if she were on the other side of Asgard, the green arrow within would show her the way home. The other three dials had not been set, and their arrows – one red, one yellow and one blue – would spin mindlessly until she specified a location. With each crown, she could set and reset different locations allowing her to create any number of combinations. On the main face was a single black arrow that always pointed north. Whenever she dared to explore outside the village, this device brought her a sense of comfort that was rivalled only by her brother's presence. With Frey now incapacitated, her father's gift was going to be relied upon more than ever before.

The mountains were three days walk. She had never journeyed that far north before, but her father had taken Frey a couple of times to trade with the gypsies that travelled in their caravans around Asgard. Twice a year, they would camp at the base of the northern mountains. Villagers that were within the area would make the trek to obtain cloth and spices from the nomadic tribe.

Her brother had thus expanded their map, and she could see that only the Terracotta Forest stood between her village and the mountains. According to Frey, the forest was so named because the soil from which the trees grew was a deep, reddish brown, and the trunks of the Terracotta trees held a stunning auburn sheen that contrasted against the yellow leaves that sprouted from their branches.

Her father had once said the forest should have been named the Gold Forest because the leaves were always golden and never green. However, it would have resulted in many an Asgardian digging there for gold when no gold had ever been found within the rich red earth. In spite of that, the trees were an excellent source of wood used by craftsmen to make furniture, art, tools, and weapons. The famous terracotta bows prized by Asgardian archers were so named because they were made from this forest.

Two rivers ran through the forest, and both met up in a fork at the boundary between the forest and mountains. All she needed to do was follow one of the rivers, and it would lead the way to her destination.

Everything appeared straightforward, but like weeds in a garden, the problems that surfaced were numerous. Freyja rubbed the sleep out of her eyes and ran over all the risks that sprouted in her head. The first problem was her mother. There was no way Nerthus was going to permit Freyja to make such a treacherous journey, but her current incapacitation would mean sneaking out would be easy. She would leave a letter explaining her actions, but Freyja feared that the precarious state of her mother's mind would be pushed over the edge.

The second problem was that the forest was an unknown. Frey had said that travelling during the day was best. At night, he took turns with father to keep watch against bandits and forest creatures that hunted under the cover of darkness. During the warmer seasons, she camped with her brother on the hill and even knew how to start a fire with flint and steel, but the idea of defending herself against potential predators froze her heart.

Then came the final and largest problem of all. Even if she managed to survive the forest and reach the mountains, the map provided no detail of where any dwarven mines resided. Looking at the blank space on the scroll was like dropping a pebble into a pond and seeing how many ripples occurred. She had to find a mine, see if any dwarves were still working in there, ask if they had unearthed any brisingr stones, and then negotiate its sale in trade somehow.

These ripples looked more like giant waves coming in from the shore to crash down upon little Freyja. She ran her hand over the map and thought of Frey lying in the next room. He would be letting out soft moans of agony, the tetanarium eating away at the last vestiges of his once healthy, vibrant and strong frame. His mind and soul taken away to some hellish place from which he would never awaken. The thought steeled her resolve. Yes, the problems were large and perhaps beyond her capabilities, but to sit back and do nothing, to not even try, was something for which she would never be able to forgive herself.

Freyja dressed and ate her breakfast without tasting her food. Her mother was in Frey's room. She was washing him down with a damp cloth, and attempting to get him to sip some soup into his emaciated body. That was the routine now for every parent with a sick child; bringing what little comfort they could and praying for a miracle.

Freyja wrote a short note and left it on the kitchen table. She was going to visit Blacksmith Gudbrand's son, Torsten, and would be back before lunch. As an afterthought, she added to the note that she would be wearing her heavy fur cloak, thick boots, and gloves, so her mother needn't worry.

The quiet morning greeted Freyja with a stillness that was unnerving, her footprints the first to mark the perfect white canvas. Deep down she knew it was all a matter of one step at a time.

The solution to the forest required Torsten. Her mind was fixed on what she might encounter in those mysterious woods. It was no use to think of how Nerthus would react to her going on such a dangerous quest. She would have to sneak out of the village and hope her mother would not feel betrayed. There was no other way around it, and she ignored the guilt that weighed her down.

Perhaps if she could get Torsten to aid her, she could get him to also leave a letter to his father, asking him to care for Nerthus and Frey in her absence.

As her boots crunched the snow, Freyja pulled out her compass and looked at the black arrow that pointed north to where the mountains lay. The arrow wobbled as she turned a corner to head toward Torsten's home, but there was no doubt which direction she needed to take to get to where the brisingr stones hopefully resided.

She smiled to herself, reassured by the compass in her hand, and unaware that eyes were watching her trudge down the snow laden path.

Old man Folke sipped the hot cup of tinkleberry tea in his hand and peered through the window. His squinty eyes followed Freyja's movements, the fingers of his other hand drummed against the wooden window sill while his expression remained a mystery.

Chapter 4

The Protector

Torsten was Frey's best friend. It also helped that he was infatuated with Freyja. He had done well to hide his true feelings because, at first, she thought he only enjoyed torturing her. From the beginning, Torsten teased her for being so shy and always hiding in Frey's shadow.

"Little mouse, you are of age now," he had said on her fourteenth summer. "You are called to be a shield-maiden of Odin, but I don't think it is our All-Father's intent that you use your brother as a shield."

Knowing how much she depended on her twin brother for security, Torsten appeared to derive great joy in stealing Frey away and doing what all boys do. Whether it was fighting with swords, working with Torsten's father in the smithy, or getting up to mischief by stealing tinkleberry pies from Lady Brenna's bakery, the pair were as thick as thieves, and Freyja always found herself chasing after them.

When the moon festival arrived and the villagers gathered to celebrate the union of Asmund and Asta with food, wine and song, Torsten would grab her by the hand without glamour or permission for the first dance. It was tradition for all the boys to have at least one dance with one of the village girls, which they hated for they preferred to eat and drink. Torsten told her he wanted to get the dance out of the way, so he could return to his friends. When she eventually built up enough courage to tell Frey of her frustrations, he burst out laughing causing her cheeks to burn.

"Oh, little sister, you are so clueless," he said, wiping a gleeful tear from his eye. His lack of sympathy left her speechless. "Do you not see he *likes* you?"

Freyja stared at her brother blankly.

"He teases but is the first to defend you if someone else tries to do the same," said Frey. "Though he says he doesn't want you to tag along when we run off to play, he always makes sure we don't leave you behind when you are breathless from chasing us. And when the moon festival dance arrives, and he wishes his duty to dance with a girl over, he always chooses his one dance with you. Not any of the other village girls. Have you not noticed this?"

As the words sank in, Freyja's cheeks burned even more. From that moment on, she never feared

Torsten would take Frey away from her. With each passing year, she noticed their moon festival dance went slightly longer, their movements a little slower, and he held her a tiny bit closer. Torsten never expressed his actual feelings, but his actions showed how true her brother's words were.

Thus, when Freyja turned to the blacksmith's son and confided her intentions to seek the brisingr stone, she was surprised by his reaction.

"Little mouse, are you out of your mind?" asked Torsten, placing a heavy hammer against an anvil. "You will not survive one day in those mountains, let alone the three days it will take to get there."

"That is why I have come to you. You can handle sword and shield, and I have seen you hunt with bow and arrow. I need you as my protector," said Freyja. She noticed that Gudbrand allowed his son to work in the smithy, but Torsten was covered from head to toe in leather clothing. A thick brown leather tunic with long sleeves, black gloves, leggings, and hardened leather boots, ensured he was protected from any accidental scratch and the dreaded tetanarium. Even his head was covered by a tight leather hood, and a thick cloth mask placed over his mouth. He had removed these though to speak to her.

For a moment, she could see him moved by the idea. His lips were a thin line of disapproval, and his black bangs could not hide the frown that creased his forehead, but his golden, brown eyes revealed how much he wished to protect her. He shook his head, refusing to be seduced by her pleas. "No, this is foolishness," he replied. "What has your mother said? She must disagree with this." When Freyja looked away, his eyes flashed angrily. "Your mother does not know?"

"We would need to sneak away," she replied. "I thought we could leave letters explaining –"

"Nonsense," interrupted Torsten, raising his hands in the air. "Your father will return with the brisingr stone."

The words sparked a fire in her belly. "Do you have Odin's eye?" asked Freyja. "You cannot divine the future. It has been over ten days since my father left, and still he has not returned. I do not wish to think what may have caused him such delay. My fear grows each day the sun sets, and he does not appear over the rise of the hill. I have waited as long as I can bear."

The sudden display of conviction caused Torsten to pause in his tirade.

"I cannot sit idly by while Frey wastes away," she added. "He is not only my brother, but he is your best friend. We must at least try."

Torsten took off his gloves and wrung his hands. "I don't know little mouse. There are still too many unknowns with your plan," he said. His voice was soft, as if not wanting to deflate this new Freyja before him. This new Freyja who was finally tapping into her own inner strength.

She grabbed both of Torsten's hands into her own, pulling his clenched fingers open and forcing them to relax. "If it was I who was struck by the tetanarium, lying in that bed filled with fevers, pain and nightmares, and my brother came to you with this plan, would you go?" she asked, a resolve passing through her palms into his.

Torsten looked deep into Freyja's sky-blue eyes. The morning sun filtered in through the smithy windows. Flashes of amber reflected in her gaze, causing the blacksmith's son to swallow hard. "I would," he answered.

"Then we leave tonight. Pack what you need, and meet me at the south gate once your parents have gone to bed."

"I do not like the deception," said Torsten.

"I do not like it either, but they would never allow us," said Freyja, biting her bottom lip. "The time taken to gather the elders, and decide whether the village can send another party to seek my father could take days, and that is time we cannot waste."

"What should the letters we leave say?" he asked.

"We are in luck. The gypsies will be arriving soon at the northern edges of the Terracotta Forest to set up their tents in preparation for the upcoming moon festival. Our letters should say we have gone to seek their aid. Given they travel all over Asgard, they may have medicines that can help fight the tetanarium.

"I have given thought that it would be wise to see the gypsies first. If they have no cure then we can move on to the mountains, and seek out the brisingr stone. This way we speak the truth about the gypsies but leave out the stone."

Torsten's lips became a hard line again. "They will see through this and divine our true intent, but we will have a good head start if they decide to chase us down." He gave Freyja's hands a squeeze then let go. "I am committed, little mouse. Let the preparations begin."

*   *   *

As she sat by her brother's side, Freyja could feel her mother's eyes looking on from the bedroom door. Amongst doing the household chores that day, Freyja had spent every free moment packing her gear without raising suspicion. Now, as she did every afternoon since her father had left, she sat holding Frey's limp hand and looked out the window. Though her body was still, her mind raced at the idea of undertaking a quest that she would never have contemplated before, especially without Frey beside her.

When dusk arrived, she listened as her mother walked away on the creaky floorboards towards her own ritual. Soon she would be in her chair downstairs, rocking back and forth, and mumbling words as if in a trance. Her mother's depression was another reason for Freyja to act. If the tetanarium was eating away at her brother's body then it was doing the equivalent to her mother's mind. Freyja knew how that felt because the waiting was causing her to go crazy also.

She pulled out her travel clothes and pack hidden under Frey's bed. The secrecy of her actions caused her body to shake as she changed. A nervous energy rippled down her spine. It made it difficult to don her green breeches, white linen shirt, woollen scarf and mittens. By the time she shoved her feet into her brown leather boots and tied its laces, it was dark outside. Torsten would already be at the gates waiting.

Fumbling with the clip on her heavy fur cloak, Freyja sought to calm her nerves by checking her belt pouches, which contained the map and magic compass. With a heavy heart, she left the letter to her mother on Frey's bedside table, and with one final kiss on her brother's cheek, she said, "Next time I see you, we will watch Asmund place his halo over Asta. Hold on and wait for me Frey."

She walked with as much stealth as she could down the stairs and out the door before letting out a tearful sob. The night air was cold as steamy puffs of her breath escaped into the night sky. The smell of wood burning in fireplaces and hot broths in pots wafted up through chimneys in village homes.

Gathering her will, Freyja headed toward the south gate. When she arrived, Torsten was already there as predicted. With a bow slung across his chest, a small round shield strapped to his back, and a long sword sheathed to his waist, he looked ready for battle, but the hooded green cloak he wore could not hide his expression of uncertainty. "I think I've packed everything we might need. Rope, flint, tinder, torches," he said, ticking them off his fingers. "Blankets, tent, waterskin…"

"What have we here?" rumbled a voice as a giant figure emerged from the shadows. Freyja let out a squeal of fright. Folke stood before them like an enormous gate barring their exit. "A bit late for a stroll outside the village, I would say." With a click of his tongue, which sounded to Freyja like a lock fastening in place, Folke bent down and grinned. "And by the looks of these packs on your back, you have enough food for quite a long stroll indeed."

Chapter 5

Water Blossom Pea Tree

Freyja and Torsten glanced sideways at each other, their mouths dry at the sudden appearance of old man Folke. Freyja's insides froze, and her hopes plummeted. Would their journey end before it even begun?

"The daughter of Njord and the son of a blacksmith, out after dark. What to make of this?" asked Folke. His eyes sparkled in a mischievous way. "A secret rendezvous between wee lovers? With travel packs so full perhaps they seek to elope?"

Freyja stared at Folke wondering what he was going on about. The old man was not so senile to not figure out what they were doing. In fact, there was no doubt he knew exactly what their plan was after her visit to his home last night.

"Folke, we are…" she began but the old man raised his hand to halt her.

Looking up at the night sky, he said, "Yes, it must be so. A tryst. The impetuous desires of youth. I do remember such a time, but it was many moons ago when I was young."

Torsten looked as dumbfounded as she felt. A second attempt at explaining caused Folke's hand to stop her again. "I must pretend that I never saw this. I am but an old man. Who am I to stand in the way of young love? It is none of my business," he said, talking to himself. "I'll be on my way. Now where was I going?"

Having focused on what Folke was saying, she only now noticed a pack strapped to his back also.

"That's right," said Folke, speaking as if the only company was his own. "I wanted to go visit the gypsies. I have some delightful potions that I'm sure they'd like to trade with me. I wish they'd come more than twice a year to our parts but Asgard is large, and I should be thankful they visit us at all. Nothing like a night time stroll."

Without another word, he walked down the dirt road leaving Freyja and Torsten standing at the gate bewildered. As Folke reached a bend, he paused with a hand on his back, and said up at the moons, "This will be a long walk indeed! I shall need to find myself a walking stick to help me along my way. My back is not what it once was." Freyja watched as Folke began rummaging around the side of the road near a copse of trees looking for fallen sticks. It dawned on her that he was waiting for them to follow.

"You spoke to old man Folke about other ways to secure a brisingr stone, did you not?" asked Torsten in a whisper.

"Yes, he is the only one, other than you, I have spoken to," said Freyja.

"He does not seek to stop us," said Torsten.

"Apparently not."

"He seeks to aid us then?"

"Perhaps," answered Freyja. "His agenda is his own, but it is clear that he wishes to travel with us while not being held responsible for our actions. He pretends to journey alone."

"Then we follow. He will, at the very least, take us to the gypsies."

Freyja nodded as they hurried to catch up to the old man. Folke re-emerged from the copse of trees with a long, gnarled piece of wood. He tested his weight against it and seemed satisfied. Without acknowledging the presence of the two young ones, he said to himself, "A day to reach the Terracotta Forest, a day to reach the northern edges, and gypsy tents should appear on the morning of the third day. I best not waste any more time on bits of wood."

Freyja and Torsten couldn't manage any words as they sought to keep up with the long strides of the old man. Folke set a pace that even the young would have been impressed with.

*   *   *

The gentle rolling hills that folded out from the village allowed for smooth passage during the night. Freyja would have enjoyed following the river that looked alive from the reflected twinkling stars overhead, but Folke moved as if Jormungandr, the world serpent, was chasing him.

One of the advantages of tending to hide in the background is it allows you to observe people better, and Freyja was quite adept in this area. With her brother stepping forward in most things, Freyja was used to standing in the shadows and watching people. She found it quite remarkable how a person could say one thing, but their expressions or movements would mean another. A twitch of the corner of the mouth, folding of arms over the chest, clenching of hands, a raised eyebrow, a forced laugh, or flushing cheeks were all physical cues that could convey how a person felt beneath the surface. The biggest tell-tale sign of all though was always the eyes. Freyja had seen many a person hide their pain behind strong words, but their eyes would betray them.

This was never more evident than when she looked at Folke. The medicine man spoke of

visiting gypsies and casual strolls, but his eyes now
contained the same urgency she had expressed to
him. The night she sought his guidance on finding a
brisingr stone, she revealed her torment and
impatience. He had said that he was no warrior, and
that the idea of seeking the dwarves for the stone
was foolishness, yet here he was heading north.
Freyja could see that his inability to cure the
children was eating away at him more than he cared
to admit, and perhaps her pleas had spurned him
into action. He still frightened her, but his actions
shone a new light on how she perceived him.

When Folke stopped to make camp, Freyja and
Torsten welcomed the break, collapsing on the
pebbly river bank in a heap. By the time the pair
gathered their breath, and slid their packs off sore
shoulders, Folke had pitched his tent and gone in
without assisting them in any way.

Whatever the reason, the charade was going to
persist. Freyja wondered how long Folke intended
to turn a blind eye to his travelling companions
before acknowledging their existence once more.
Torsten shrugged his shoulders in answer to her
unspoken question and went about getting their own
tents ready while she started a campfire.

Thankfully the snow was not falling for a second
night, so Freyja was able to get a cheery fire going.

She went to fetch some water from the river and returned to the smells of sausages sizzling in a pan. Torsten poked them to prevent them from burning, and they ate their dinner and spoke in hushed tones. Their conversation centred on Folke, and what he was seeking to achieve by coming along. The discussion ended with more questions than answers and left Freyja feeling drained. When Torsten asked whether he should see if Folke wanted a sausage, they were greeted by loud snores. Following his lead, they did likewise and entered their own tents. Freyja fell asleep as soon as she crawled into her bedroll and her head touched the pillow.

*   *   *

By noon the following day, they reached the edges of the Terracotta Forest. Had Torsten not woken at the crack of dawn that morning, they would have missed Folke heading off without them. As it was, Freyja was jostled awake. The pair hastily dressed, shoved their gear into packs, and ran after the old man, blurry eyed and yawning.

Freyja spent those early hours staring at the ground. Her energies concentrated on putting one aching foot in front of the other. When the dirt road began to change to a deep red clay colour, she looked up and was greeted by a brilliant sea of gold leafed trees that caused her jaw to drop open. They stood for a moment and admired the terracotta trunks that looked more stone than wood, and the giant canopy of gold, fluttering in the wind, reflecting the sunlight like burnished metal. It was easy to see how someone could believe this forest contained gold beneath its roots.

"Quite a sight, isn't it?" said Torsten.

"My father described it to me before," whispered Freyja. "But his words failed to do this place justice. It is beyond what I imagined." The winter did not penetrate the Terracotta Forest. A perpetual autumn with the scents of earth, wood and leaves that filled Freyja's lungs with a sense of life, but there was a melancholy to the atmosphere. A type of sadness that mixed in with a life that had lived an age beyond time.

Distracted by the beauty and ancient nature of the forest, Freyja did not notice that old man Folke was now walking behind her. The change in marching order also dawned on Torsten. Gently, he reached out and grabbed Freyja's arm to stop. Folke also paused, not looking at them. His face admiring the golden leaves in a way that spoke nothing of what he was thinking. The question of why he was no longer leading them caused a wave of unease to tingle down her arms.

"Take out your compass," whispered Torsten. The forest was quiet except for the wind rustling the leaves, and the sounds of the river flowing somewhere to the east, hidden by the trees.

Freyja obeyed and together they looked at the small instrument. The black arrow pointed north, the same direction they were walking and gave an assurance that was not entirely felt. The dial with the green arrow was pointing south west, back to home. The other dials had their arrows spinning because no place had been set. She was aware that one of the limits of the magical device was that it could not be set to a place it had never been to before. For instance, it had never been taken to any of the mines in the northern mountains, so Freyja had to rely on her map, and the black arrow to guide her in the right direction.

They recommenced their trek, and Freyja kept an eye on the compass as they walked deeper into the forest. The crunch of the golden leaves underfoot sounded too loud, and she tried to calm her heavy breathing. After a couple of hours of following the clay path, it opened into a small meadow. There stood a grassy knoll with a brook that ran around its side. Red and white petunias dotted the lush grass, attracting bees and butterflies. On top of the knoll stood a small tree, and a cool breeze carried the sweet scent of honey and perfume from the flowers.

"Looks like a good place to stop for lunch and fill our water-skins," said Torsten.

"It's perfect," remarked Freyja.

The pair walked up to the knoll, Freyja marvelled at the hummingbirds that flitted to and fro drinking nectar amongst the bees. She put down her pack, rubbing her neck and watched Torsten head to the brook with skins in hand. From what she could tell, the water flowed not from the river to the east but from the ground beneath the knoll. Lifting her head, she inhaled the coolness of the afternoon, savouring the moment when her heart suddenly skipped a beat.

The tree on top of the knoll that she was sitting under was a water blossom pea tree. She recognised the delicate pink flowers that littered along its branches and the fragrance they emitted. The flowers themselves were not uncommon in these parts but it occurred to her that the tree was covered in leaves of green.

Not gold.

Freyja's head snapped back as she surveyed the clearing. The boundary of terracotta trees with its gold filigree leaves stopped at the edges of the meadow, and this solitary water blossom pea tree with leaves a colour that defied the rest of the forest stood out like a sudden warning. The unease felt previously returned with a piercing arrow of panic as she realised old man Folke was nowhere to be seen.

Chapter 6

The Worthy

Freyja stood up and looked in every direction. "Folke!" she called out, but only silence was her response. She looked at her compass in some vain hope that it would point in the direction of where he had gone. "Folke!" she shouted again in earnest, unable to hide her fear. She felt dizzy, unsure if it was from the scented flowers, or her head spinning around trying to locate the old man. "Torsten! Can you see Folke? He has disappeared."

As she turned, Freyja caught the reflected light of a metal object. It was coming from the water blossom pea tree. On the trunk, she saw a plaque and approached it tentatively, her heart pounding for reasons she didn't understand. The plaque read:

- ONE -
You enter a place serene and secure
But beware the waters and their allure
For if you drink to quench your thirst
You will not waken until sun dispersed
And once the moons appear in the skies
The dead will come to claim their prize

Freyja whispered the words aloud and upon finishing, her eyes grew wide in alarm. *But beware the waters and their allure.*

"Torsten!" she cried.

She ran down the knoll and found him lying by the brook. His sprawled form unmoving as one of his hands held limply an open water-skin. *For if you drink to quench your thirst. You will not waken until sun dispersed.* Her vision blurred as she bent down and looked for signs of life. He was still breathing, but his eyes refused to open no matter how hard she shook him. Blinking back tears, she dragged Torsten away from the running waters, and pulled him under the shade of the water blossom pea tree. The blacksmith son looked like he was having an afternoon nap, his face calm and unaware of Freyja's growing distress. *And once the moons appear in the skies. The dead will come to claim their prize.*

Looking at the position of the sun, Freyja guessed there were a few hours remaining before sunset. She called out again for Folke, but it was no use, the old man refused to appear.

"Please don't shout," said a voice in her head.

Freyja spun around in fright but there was no one there.

"Don't bother looking for me."

"Folke?" asked Freyja to the voice.

"I assume that's the name of the old man that was with you. Strange he let you enter this place without warning." Freyja listened, realising the voice was not Folke's but higher pitched. It reminded her of her twin brother, though Frey's voice was less haughty than this one.

"What is this place?" said Freyja.

"You have stepped on ancient grounds. Few know how to find it. It can be a sanctuary, but also a cursed place. You did not heed the tree's warning."

"Please help me."

The voice cawed with laughter. *"Help you? If you wish my help, you will have to prove yourself worthy. I am surprised you can hear my words. That shows promise from one so young, but you will have to survive the night. I would not seek to escape with your friend, they will hunt you down. Your only hope is to solve the riddle and lift the curse."*

"What riddle?" Freyja pleaded to make sense of what was happening.

"Look on the other side of the tree."

Freyja stared at the tree and moved around it. There on the other side was another plaque. She ran her fingers over the etched words and read aloud:

- TWO -
To solve the curse you need to find
That which is identical but has no mind
It shows everything as if it is real
It can be touched but cannot feel
Upon the living it leaves no stain
But the dead cannot look without feeling pain
So find that which captures earth and sky
Sun and stars, you and I
Within its depths every detail will yield
And you can use it as your shield

Freyja read the riddle several times trying to discern its secrets. Her mind raced as she let the words stick to her lips. “I don’t understand,” she whispered.

“Then the dead will come to claim you and your friend, I’m afraid,” said the disembodied voice.

“Do you know the answer?”

“Of course. This is my creation. To discern the worthy from the unworthy.”

“You created this?” she asked without expecting an answer. “Please, can you give me some clue?”

“Do not beg, it is unsightly child. Solve the riddle, survive the night, and you will gain a most powerful ally. I will be watching.”

"Wait!" shouted Freyja, but she felt a void in her mind. The voice had gone.

*   *   *

By the time the sun touched the horizon, and the Terracotta Forest filled with long shadows and stillness, Freyja felt an overwhelming pressure upon her chest. Other than covering Torsten with a blanket where he lay, she had spent the remaining hours of daylight, walking around the water blossom pea tree. Her eyes read the plaques while her mind attempted to unravel its true meaning.

In the end, the circles she walked around the tree reflected the circles that ran around in her head. *To solve the curse you need to find. That which is identical but has no mind. It shows everything as if it is real. It can be touched but cannot feel.* From these words, she concluded that she needed to find an object as opposed to a creature or animal. An object has no mind, and it can be touched but cannot feel. The only meaning she could get from the rest of the riddle was that the object could be used to protect her against whatever would seek to kill them. She had no idea what type of object could capture the earth, sky, sun, stars, and people.

She thought perhaps it referred to Jormungandr, the world serpent, whose scaly body could wrap around Asgard. Its jaws could swallow the sun and stars, but that was a living creature that had a mind and could feel. She contemplated perhaps Odin's eye, which could capture the detail of everything it looked at whether it be celestial bodies in the sky or the people of Asgard. The eye itself also had no mind of its own, and it did not feel like a hand feels though she imagined if anyone tried to poke a stick into Odin's eye, it would feel pain. Freyja threw her arms up in disgust. Even if one of these was the answer, it was not like she could walk up to the world serpent and put a leash on it, or approach the almighty Odin and ask if she could borrow his eye.

With the sun gone, Freyja began to shiver. She stopped pacing and gathered some dry wood to start a campfire. Was it her imagination or was the air much colder than usual? Though no snow fell, Freyja felt a bitter cold, and the meadow now seemed ominous and empty. The bees, butterflies and hummingbirds had long departed the knoll. The flowers seemed to droop as if wanting to curl into themselves in protection from whatever was to come. She needed more warmth, more light. Pulling out several torches, Freyja lit them and then wedged them in a protective circle in the ground. Together with the campfire, she felt a little safer, but it couldn't prevent the sobs she had held in all afternoon.

"Why are you crying little mouse?" asked Torsten through sleepy eyes.

"Torsten!" she exclaimed with enormous relief.

"What's going on? Is it night already? I remember going to the brook to fill our skins, and I drank a mouthful cupped in my hands, but nothing else after that." Torsten sat up and yawned.

Freyja wasted no time in explaining the precarious situation they were in. It took a few minutes for Torsten to absorb what was happening. With torch in hand, they examined the plaques on the tree.

"By Odin's beard, this is beyond me," he said defeated. They returned to their campfire and the circle of torches. Torsten pulled out his bow and notched an arrow. "I know not what may come, but I know of few things that can withstand an arrow through its heart." Freyja could tell he was trying to be brave, but the slight waver in his eyes revealed the fear he was hiding. They had no idea what they were about to face.

Huddling together, they ate supper close to the campfire. Both looking beyond the aura of light from the torches, trying to discern what may lie in the darkness. "So Folke did not follow?" asked Torsten in disdain.

"I am unsure what happened to him," said Freyja. "The magic of this clearing captured our attention, and he was behind us."

"If he knew the dangers of this place, surely, he would have stopped us from entering," said Torsten between mouthfuls of cheese and bread.

Freyja shrugged. "Maybe he wandered off, while we followed this path. It does not matter. What is more pressing is what we face now."

"And this voice you heard said it would be useless for us to flee? Even though I am now awake, and you would not have to carry me?"

"I am convinced that by drinking the waters from this knoll, we have stirred whatever has been asleep, and the voice was clear that what has woken would still hunt us down, no matter how far we run." Freyja nibbled on a green apple, its sour sweetness was a welcome sensation in her mouth.

A crack of twigs caused both their heads to snap to attention. "Who goes there?" shouted Torsten, raising his bow in the direction of the noise. "Grab my sword, little mouse."

Freyja retrieved the sword from its sheath and stood close next to him holding it aloft awkwardly. It was a sharp blade but light, and Freyja guessed

Torsten chose it specifically in the event that she would have to wield a weapon.

The snapping of twigs was soon joined by the crumpling of leaves, and Freyja stood frozen in horror as pinpoints of red light started to appear in the darkness. Pairs of glowing red pupils focused on the two young Asgardians within the circle of torches. Freyja counted at least a dozen. As they sauntered toward them, her throat clenched in terror. Reaching the torch light, she saw skeletal forms come into focus. Wearing mismatched pieces of rusted armour, torn clothing and battered helmets, the undead creatures lumbered forward, their skulls and bones glowed bluish white, causing the torch flames to flicker. Freyja felt the unholy chill emanating from them and knew that to be touched by them would mean death.

Torsten let loose an arrow with a poise that belied the danger surrounding them, and the arrow pierced through the ribcage of one of the skeletons causing it to shatter into a mess of bones. The light of its red pupils dying out. With astounding precision, the blacksmith son retrieved arrows from his quiver, and fired at the undead, striking each one.

"They walk straight at us. Easy marks," said Torsten with grim satisfaction. "The ring of torches was a smart thing to do." He smiled, causing her to relax, but the reprieve was short lived. In disbelief, they watched as the scattered remains of each skeleton began to move. The bones rattled against broken armour as the undead assembled and rose once more, their glowing red eyes ablaze.

"By Odin's beard!" exclaimed Torsten. "Grab our packs and a torch. We must run." They scrambled down the side of the knoll. Freyja looked behind her. The skeletons were no longer shambling like broken derelicts but moving quicker along the icy ground. Fear caused her to trip, and she fell hard against the cold earth near the brook. How can you kill something that is already dead? She thought in dismay. Torsten planted a torch next to her, and let loose more arrows. Helplessness chewed at her mind as the skeletons drew closer. Soon Torsten's quiver would be empty, and the dead would claim their prize.

Freyja glimpsed into the waters that were the source of their tragedy. From the torch she still held, she could see her own reflection in the running brook, and without warning the riddle returned. *To solve the curse you need to find. That which is identical but has no mind.* She looked at herself again in the water. Her reflection stared back.

Identical but has no mind. *It shows everything as if it is real. It can be touched but cannot feel.*

"It fits," she whispered in disbelief. She got up on her knees and rummaged frantically through her pack.

"What are you doing?" shouted Torsten, his bow string strumming in the night as arrows flew through the air. "Run! Run!"

So find that which captures earth and sky. Sun and stars, you and I. Within its depths every detail will yield. And you can use it as your shield. From deep within her pack, Freyja pulled out a shiny object with gilded frame. She held it aloft in one hand, while the torch was in her other, and prayed to Odin. The skeletons closest to them slowed. The mirror she held reflected every detail of their demented images, and like spent coals, the glowing eyes began to shrink.

With bated breath, Freyja moved the mirror from side to side, halting each skeleton in its path. Upon seeing their reflection, they raised their bony fingers as if blinded, and with opened jaws screaming silently into the night, she and Torsten watched as they disintegrated into dust. When the last skeleton returned to the Asgardian soil, Freyja felt a presence fill a void in her mind, and listened as it said, *"Well done! Well done! You are worthy!"*

Chapter 7

Reward

Freyja awoke the next morning huddled next to Torsten. The pleasant sun shone through the meadow awakening the petunias, and ensuring the return of the bees and butterflies. Had it all been a nightmare? It was as if the horrors of the previous night never occurred, but a careful eye could spot the small mounds of grey ash where the skeletons had turned into dust. She still held the mirror in her hand, its gilded frame dug into her skin because she had gripped it too hard. Part of her still could not believe that the reflection it produced stopped the undead from claiming them.

"You have finally awakened," said the voice in Freyja's head.

She looked around not expecting to see the source of the disembodied voice, but found her attention caught by the movement of wings. There perched in the water blossom pea tree was a small bird, its breast the colour of snow, and its silver wings thin and tapered like the blades of a throwing knife. Its head darted from side to side before its eyes settled on Freyja.

"To think that a child as timid as the petunias within this meadow has succeeded where so many others have perished," said the voice, which Freyja knew came from the bird, though she could not explain how.

"Who are you?" She sent the question out from her mind.

"My name is Hemming," said the bird. *"I am a falcon first and foremost, and a creation of the All-father. You have accomplished a feat that I have waited eons for, you have passed an Odin test."*

"An Odin test?"

The falcon nipped under its wing with its sharp beak. *"Yes. Throughout Asgard, the All-father has created tests to seek those with potential. His eye can catch glimpses of the worthy, but it is never clear looking into the fog of the future."*

"For what purpose?"

"All in good time child," said Hemming. *"You know it is rude for one to withhold their name when the other has freely given it."*

"I'm sorry, it's Freyja," she whispered, not wanting to wake Torsten who was still snoring.

"Very good. Thus, the bond is complete," said Hemming. *"You will find me a most powerful ally if you use me wisely."*

"I don't quite understand." Freyja looked at the falcon, a crinkle crossing her brow.

The falcon ruffled its wings in annoyance. *"You may, if you wish, think of me as a reward for passing the Odin test, but I am a living creature with beating heart in my breast. I do have a will of my own and though I am bound to you, it does not mean you can take advantage of our partnership."*

"I... I see." Her thoughts stuttered as she raised her hands in supplication.

"You are wasting time child." Hemming launched off the branch and landed on Freyja's shoulder. Claws dug into her cloak and caused her to flinch. *"Now we are bound, I know the purpose of your journey, and the disease that plagues your village. I have flown the northern reaches of the Terracotta Forest and can confirm the gypsies have arrived. You best wake that sleepy head next to you if you wish to reach the gypsy tents by nightfall. Allow me to scout ahead and provide safe passage."*

Freyja grappled with this strange turn of events as Hemming detached and flew towards a northern path obscured by trees. Shaking Torsten awake, she had no idea how she was going to explain that a magical falcon was now her friend.

*   *   *

Torsten thought Freyja had knocked her head after their battle against the undead. He was only convinced of Hemming's existence when he watched the falcon drop down from the sky between two large trees and land on Freyja's outstretched arm. She had donned a thick leather glove that ran past her elbow, which provided more protection from Hemming's claws than her soft, woolly cloak. Torsten had a long staring match with the falcon, which he inevitably lost.

"I'm not sure what you see in this young fellow," said Hemming. *"Has he never seen a bird before?"*

"I think he's struggling with the part where you and I can communicate with our minds." Freyja gave a reassuring smile to Torsten, and he responded with an uneasy grin.

"Well, tell him to stop staring."

Freyja let out a chuckle. *"I don't think you fully grasp the magnitude of your presence Hemming."*

"I know I am awe inspiring, but it's rude to stare," said Hemming. *"Anyway, this path leads north and then north-east after a league. You'll merge next to the river and follow it until you see a bridge. Cross it and the path on the other side will take you straight to the gypsies. There were no signs*

of any trouble that I could see, and I can see a fair way."

"Thank you Hemming."

"Oh, and that old man Folke is behind you again."

"What???"

Freyja spun around, grabbing Torsten's arm in the process. Together they watched as the lumbering form of old man Folke came trundling up with walking stick in hand. With a jovial smile spread across his face, he strolled past them as if they were young saplings rooted to the spot.

"Folke!" shouted Freyja, a surprising note of anger in her voice. "Where have you been? Where were you last night? We were almost killed!"

The old man stopped a short distance from them and bent down to examine the base of a Terracotta tree with mushrooms surrounding it. "So many wonderful plants in this forest," he said to himself as he picked several flat-topped fungi. "Some for potent potions, others for hearty stews. Which one could you be used for, I wonder?" He put the mushroom to his bulbous nose and smelled it before breaking a small piece and popping it into his mouth. "Stew!" he answered happily.

As he pocketed the mushrooms into a pouch, Torsten moved over to block his path. Folke was twice the size of Torsten, but the young man remained defiant, hands on his hips, demanding the old man's attention.

Folke looked up at the clear winter sky and said, "There may not be gold in this forest, but I've always believed there are far greater gifts this place holds." He took a sideways step around Torsten and added to no one in particular, "But only to those who are worthy. I really must stop dawdling and see those gypsies. I have so many ingredients now to trade with them."

Freyja stared at Folke as he continued on while whistling a tune, her thoughts undeniably wondering what game the old man was playing.

*   *   *

Hemming's directions were accurate, and by late afternoon, they saw coloured flags peeking above the canopy of trees. When the forest opened, a line of patchwork tents pitched into the ground, and caravans on wooden wheels with stained glass windows and brick chimneys came into view.

Freyja wished she had more eyes so she could capture the entire scene. Each tent was like a giant quilt. Large square pieces of coloured canvas stitched together in a chaotic ensemble to form unique patterns. A giant flagpole displayed an emblem of each gypsy family. Dragons, pixies, bears, fish, unicorns, snakes, and many other creatures were stitched into each flag as they fluttered in the wind.

The caravans displayed designs that gave hints as to what that gypsy family traded in. One had birds painted over it like an aviary, another had bubbling cauldrons and potion bottles depicted on its sides, and yet another had a crystal ball and tarot cards splashed along its walls. Sure enough, looking in each tent confirmed the speciality of that gypsy family was what was illustrated on their caravan.

Freyja poked her head into the giant tent next to the caravan that looked like an aviary. She gasped in wonder at all the different types of birds flying from wooden perches set up within. She wanted nothing more than to examine each one, but she shook her head as thoughts returned to Frey lying sick back home.

"Hemming, are you able to fly over this area and locate a gypsy that may assist us?" She looked at the falcon sitting on her shoulder, nuzzling against her neck.

"Of course, I can fly over this area," he replied. *"Whether I can find a gypsy that has a cure for the*

tetanarium is another question entirely, but I will be back shortly."

"There goes Folke wandering into that tent attached to the caravan with the tarot cards," said Torsten with disgust.

"It is clear we cannot depend on him," said Freyja. "We must plan our steps as if he was not here."

"He isn't half the time," replied Torsten. "But you are right. We do this on our own. So where do we start?"

"I have asked Hemming to fly overhead and see if he can spy a tent that may help us. In the meantime, perhaps we try that tent with the caravan that has potion bottles painted over it."

They entered the potions tent but re-emerged without success. "They sell love potions and brain elixirs that make you smarter," scoffed Torsten. "The day those things work will be the day I lift Thor's hammer."

"Yes, I doubt their authenticity," agreed Freyja. She heard a falcon cry and watched as Hemming soared lazily back to her from up high.

"Walk east child. There is a caravan with gemstones painted over it with a chequered purple and orange tent," said the falcon.

"Do you think they have what we need?" The words ushered forth with a well of hope.

"I do not know. The tent flap is closed, and I could not fly in."

Freyja grabbed Torsten's hand and ran east. The blacksmith son looked on bewildered but let her lead the way. She spotted the caravan first. Rubies, emeralds, sapphires, diamonds, and many other stones were splashed all over it in a dizzying array of painted colour. The chequered tent looked pale in comparison even though it took up a space twice the size of the caravan. As Freyja lifted the flap and entered, she held her breath and prayed that somewhere inside lay the elusive brisingr stone.

Chapter 8

Gypsies of Asgard

There was an expectation the tent would be filled with glass cabinets of jewellery, large wooden chests overflowing with gemstones, or shelves of precious treasures upon entering. Instead, Freyja was greeted by a tent empty except for a single wooden table with a square lit lantern on top of it.

Sitting on a high chair at the table was a little man with a blue handkerchief wrapped around his head. Shocks of purple hair stood out in every direction like he had been struck by lightning. Glasses with round yellow lenses were perched on a very pointy nose, and his legs dangled off the floor. His chubby hands were busy shuffling through pieces of parchment spread out in front of him, and a feathered quill the length of his short arm was dipped into an ink bottle before making scribbles on select documents.

Without taking his eyes off the parchments, the little man said, "Welcome to House Orios, gnome gypsy and trader of fine gems, rings, bracelets, necklaces, amulets, and rare artefacts. My name is Panagem Orios, but everyone calls me Pan. How can I help you today?" He said all this in one breath, and Freyja suspected it was an introduction spoken a hundred times before.

In her clearest voice, she was about to ask whether Pan sold brisingr stones when the gnome pointed his quill at Freyja. "I'll give you two rubies for that falcon," he said without raising his head.

"Don't you even think about selling me child, or I'll claw your eyes out," said Hemming without a hint of humour.

"I would never sell you." Freyja looked at the falcon horrified.

"Don't tell me, tell the gnome," said Hemming.

"The falcon is not for sale," she stammered at Pan.

"Very well," he said. "I'll give you twenty pieces of gold for the magic compass in your left pocket, ten gold for the boy's bow, he can keep the arrows, five gold for his sword, and five silver for the round shield. There is nothing else you have that I want."

Freyja and Torsten looked at each other dumbfounded, unable to explain how Pan could see the items they owned with his head buried in ink and paper. Even if he was looking at them, how could he know that Freyja carried a magic compass hidden in her pocket?

For someone with such slight stature, Freyja found Pan an imposing figure. "I'm sorry, you misunderstand. I'm here to buy not sell," she chirped.

This caused Pan to put down his quill and parchment. The yellow lenses on his glasses reflected the lantern light as he revealed a large smile. Several of Pan's teeth were gold, which made Freyja feel uneasy. "Oh really?" asked Pan. "Unless you wish to use that bird as payment, I doubt you can afford anything I have for sale."

"Maybe if I peck out those gold nuggets he uses for teeth, we can buy something," suggested Hemming.

"Don't you dare!" Freyja looked at the falcon wide eyed. She reached out a soothing hand and stroked the feathers on Hemming's back.

"Just say the word," said Hemming. *"This gnome needs to learn I am no object to be bought and sold."*

Freyja ignored Hemming's voice and returned her attention to the gnome. "I am after a specific gem called the brisingr stone," she said.

"And if I had one, how would you pay for it?" asked Pan.

"What would it cost?" countered Freyja.

"More than the two of you combined. Even if you threw in the bird that wouldn't be enough," said the bemused gnome. "You ask for a stone that in all my journeys around Asgard, I have seen but a handful of times, and those who possess such a stone have never sold it to me. So, you're out of luck. Not even I carry such a stone. Those that Skadi the Jotunn does not hoard would be kept by the dwarves, and if you think my prices are unfair, wait until you barter with them. If you manage to find one."

Freyja's hopes plummeted. She carried with her a small pouch of coin. Money that she had earned from working at the bakery and picking fruit in the orchards over many months. Torsten had also given his earnings from working in the blacksmith, and combined they managed sixteen pieces of gold, twelve pieces of silver, and twenty pieces of copper. She had hoped that was enough to purchase one small brisingr stone, but Pan was clear they were worth much more.

It also meant there was no other choice but to journey on to the northern mountains, and somehow find the dwarves, assuming they still worked the mines. Now that they had traversed the Terracotta Forest, the problem of the mountains loomed much larger.

"Do you have anything that the dwarves would exchange the brisingr stone for?" she asked.

The gnome stared at Freyja, hands shaped together like a steeple, and his fingers tapping against pursed lips. "You're persistent I must say," said Pan. "I do own several artefacts that the dwarves would part a brisingr stone for, but those items are far more valuable than the stone itself. You do not have enough coin for a single stone let alone one of those artefacts."

"Can you at least tell me what they are?" pleaded Freyja.

Pan continued to stare, weighing up her words. "I like you," he eventually responded. "So, I'll do better than tell you, I'll show you. Follow me." Without preamble, he hopped off his high chair, and with surprising speed for one with such short legs, he scurried over to the rear of the tent. Leaning against the canvas was a long pole with a metal hook. With skilful precision, he raised the pole, and placed the hook over a metal clasp sewn almost invisibly into the tent. He pulled down, releasing the clasp, and held the revealed flap open while Freyja and Torsten were ushered through.

The tent connected to the gypsy's caravan, and Freyja approached the wooden steps that led up to its door. Digging into his pocket, Pan fished out a metal ring with more keys than Freyja had ever seen before. There were at least a hundred of them, but the gnome found the key he needed almost immediately and opened the door. Inside, their eyes fell upon a large room with polished mahogany cabinets running along the length and breadth of every wall.

Freyja had experienced Asgardian magic in small amounts. Torsten's father knew of some simple runes that when etched on metal would cause it to glow. A useful bit of magic to inscribe upon a sword or shield to act as a light in darkness, and allow the wielder to not bother with a lantern. In the past, when blacksmith Gudbrand performed the ritual, she felt the magic energy pulse through her veins and cause her skin to be covered in gooseflesh.

However, walking into Pan's caravan, Freyja was bombarded by magical energy. It coursed through her body and caused the tips of her hair to lift in the air. The impact was overwhelming, and she grabbed the edge of the doorway to steady herself.

"The magic emanates from the cabinets," said Hemming, fluttering his wings as if shaking off dust. *"Thieves could not easily unlock them without risking their lives."*

Torsten swallowed hard as if suffering from a dry mouth. It was clear that even though he worked the furnaces with his father, he too never experienced such magic contained in one place.

Pan smiled revealing his gold teeth again, pleased to see the effect his home was having on the two young visitors. Flipping through his ring of keys, he stopped at a small silver one, which he inserted into a keyhole between two cabinets. As soon as he turned it Freyja gasped in surprise, for each mahogany cabinet began to glow and then become transparent. They now looked like glass and revealed the abundance of treasures within.

Pan stepped over to one of the mahogany-now-glass cabinets. "This diamond tipped spade is imbued with old Jotunn magic. It allows the user to locate water hidden underground. A most useful tool when mining. If you happen to become trapped and need water to survive, this spade will penetrate through soil and rock like butter, and pull the user toward fresh water." He walked over to another cabinet. "This item looks like an ordinary candle but is imbued with the light of Heimdallr, guardian of the Bifrost, and he who is known as the one who illuminates the world. This candle never goes down, its wax never melts and thus can provide light in the darkest of places until the end days of Ragnarök.

These are a couple of artefacts that any mining dwarf would love to get their hands on."

Freyja marvelled at them and browsed through the plethora of gems, jewellery, and magic items with ingenuous fascination. How long must it have taken for Pan to acquire such treasure? Amidst the dazzling displays, her eye caught a tiny twinkle. Moving over to one of the corners of the caravan, she spied sitting on a velvet pillow, a solitary silver needle. It looked like an ordinary sewing needle and of little value compared to the rest of Pan's collection.

"You have an eye for the subtle," observed the gypsy, strolling over next to her. "I bought that from an old goblin seamstress. She was a kooky soul but had exceptional skill for elaborate dress. This needle can mend any tear and can sew any material together. It has been infused with goblin magic, which is volatile and unpredictable so I'm not sure how well it really works."

"How much?" asked Freyja.

Pan looked up at her surprised. "No dwarf will want this. You won't get a brisingr stone for it."

Freyja bent down, her nose almost touching the cabinet display as she examined the needle. She closed her eyes and sensed the strange goblin magic. It was different to other magic and instead of coursing through her veins, settled on her tongue of all places. It was a bizarre sensation that she tasted rather than felt, and the taste was sweet like flowing honey. Not knowing why, she imagined moistening yarn with her tongue and threading it through the eye of the silver needle.

"How much?" repeated Freyja.

Pan's glasses flashed, his own interest piqued. "I'll trade you the bird for the needle," he said.

"My child," interrupted Hemming. *"I believe Pan's spectacles do more than allow the wearer to see clearly. In fact, I am positive they bring into focus the true nature of things. And that includes myself. I would not be surprised if Pan knows I am a creation of the All-father and come from an Odin test."*

Freyja pretended to consider the offer before answering. "I told you Pan, my falcon is not for sale," she said.

Pan feigned a look of ignorance. "My apologies." The gnome paused in thought. "How about this? I will give you the needle in exchange for your hair."

It was Freyja's turn to look surprised. "My hair?"

"Not all of it," said Pan. "Just the bottom half. We'll cut it off say to your shoulders. Do we have a deal? It is not like it won't grow back."

"He does know you have completed an Odin test!" said Hemming. The falcon's voice rang loud in Freyja's mind. *"He knows you are an Asgardian with potential. He does not know what you will become, but by asking for your hair, he seeks to obtain your properties."*

"By giving my hair, can he hurt me?" Freyja tried to remain calm as she glanced at the falcon.

"Unlikely, he will not use your hair until you are older. It is like Heimdallr's candle, he may infuse in objects the magical properties contained within your hair," answered Hemming. *"What those exact properties are will not be known until your potential is realised."*

Freyja absorbed the falcon's words and looked at the needle again. "You have a deal," she said.

"Are you sure about this?" whispered Torsten in her ear. He observed the exchange without a word but now felt the need to intervene. "It's a sewing needle. Can't see much use for it, and why would Pan want your hair? I don't trust him."

Freyja squeezed Torsten's hand. "It's only hair," she said.

"Excellent," said Pan as he walked over to a counter and retrieved some scissors.

A short while later, Freyja departed a good head of hair lighter. In her pouch, next to her magic compass, lay the silver needle tucked into its velvet pillow. She did not know what strange force compelled her to buy the needle, but for whatever reason, she did feel she had struck the better deal.

Chapter 9

Mountain Puzzle

Outside the tent, Freyja found the large frame of old man Folke standing like a thick trunk flagpole. He was reading an ancient tome with frail gold leaf pages while smoking a long pipe. Freyja tried to make out the title on the cover, but whatever words were there had long since faded. Seeing her emerge, he said, "Why if it isn't young Freyja, and Torsten the blacksmith apprentice. Fancy meeting you here."

Torsten stepped forward. "Enough with the charade Folke. We traversed the Terracotta forest and reached the gypsies, no thanks to you, and now we move on to the northern mountains," he said. "You know we seek the brisingr stone, so you can either help us or get out of our way."

"I made a very good trade for this book," remarked Folke, patting the tome's cover. "So, I'm in a pleasant mood and will overlook such disrespectful talk, my lad." He slapped a large hand on the blacksmith son's shoulder, causing Torsten to wince. "Otherwise, I might have to teach you some manners and scrub that tongue with hard soap."

Freyja attempted to calm the situation down and said, "Please help us. Our quest is noble, you surely see that."

Folke let go and rolled the tongue in his mouth considering Freyja's plea. Torsten rubbed his shoulder and gave the old man a dark look. "Why do the youth always think they know better than their elders? As if somehow, the years of experience they *don't* have makes them wiser?" asked Folke. The question wasn't aimed so much at Freyja as it was to all young Asgardians in general. "You go north to find dwarves. The mountains are riddled with mines, tunnels strewn in a maze only those greedy creatures, and perhaps ants, could follow without getting lost. Most of them will be abandoned. The dwarves moved on to other rock kingdoms in Asgard. I will join you only because I want to see your faces when you realise the futility of the task and go running back home with your wee tails between your legs."

Freyja could not refute the old man's claims. The steps taken to reach this point required all the courage she could muster, and now she reached a point where placing one foot in front of the other wasn't going to be enough. It was like arriving at a canyon without a bridge and being asked to jump across it.

Wilting under Folke's smirk, Freyja turned to Torsten and said, "We still have some daylight. Let's try to cover as much ground as possible. The map indicates the first rise of the mountains are not far from where we are." Torsten nodded and they headed off, ignoring Folke as he lumbered behind them.

Freyja focused on her compass, hoping it would reveal much more than an arrow pointing north. The old man's words echoed inside her head, taunting hopes and elevating fears. If she gave up now, it meant returning to Frey's bedside with empty hands and shattered dreams. There had to be a way to locate the dwarves. It was a problem she needed to confront, and it was no use worrying if she failed.

By the time the last caravan was obscured by the trees, and only the gypsy flags could be seen poking through to the skies above, Freyja barely registered her surroundings. As they marched north, not even one final comment from Folke distracted her as he shouted from the rear, "Oh and I must say, that's one mighty fine bird you have there."

*   *   *

The ground transformed from terracotta clay to hard soil and brown rock as they continued toward their destination. The trail they followed was now covered in gravel, and the bushes and foliage became sparse. The river could now be seen and looked like brittle metal against grey skies. The current was strong, and Freyja doubted she could survive a crossing in those icy waters.

They wound their way northward and stopped before a low cliff that rose before them. Having spent the entire time seeking a solution to the problem of finding the dwarves, Freyja was surprised to see a waterfall descending from the top of the cliff to form in a pool that connected to the river below. She imagined during a warmer season, it would be a perfect spot to have a picnic and a swim.

Torsten pointed to the side of the waterfall. "Over there, a staircase etched into the rock. We can ascend there," he said. The steep weathered stairs were slippery and moss-covered from the spray of the waterfall, and Freyja used her hands for extra security. It was like climbing an unsafe ladder, where each foothold could lead to a misstep and a dangerous plummet. She let out an exhausted breath when they reached the top.

Where before the cliff blocked her view, she now could see the river run like a slithering snake toward the base of the northern mountains. To the east, she spied the other river that ran through the Terracotta forest and followed it northward until it joined at a fork with the west river.

Freyja had been so lost in thought that she did not realise how elevated they were until she turned and saw they were above the tree line. With the sun lowering toward the horizon, and the winds coming from the west, the forest erupted like burnished metal. A sea of shimmering rose gold leaves that flowed and ebbed like endless waves of molten brilliance.

Bright coloured flags and the patchwork tents of the gypsies could be seen on the forest's edge. The encampment looked like the toy models her brother played with when he was a child. Beyond her sight, somewhere far south was her village, and the many children trapped in feverish nightmares. Freyja gulped in the air, never thinking she could come this far and knowing there was still further to go.

"There is still enough light for us to follow the river and reach the mountain's base. We can make camp there if we hurry," said Torsten, admiring the view next to her.

Freyja didn't want to look at the gigantic obstacle before her. The thought of aimlessly exploring the warren of mines diminished her courage, but any hope of finding a brisingr stone was buried somewhere in that enormous chunk of ice and rock.

In the waning sunlight, the mountain range cast a dark blanket over the forest that showed Folke had not exaggerated their plight. The side of the mountain closest to her looked like the world serpent, Jormungandr, had bitten into it several times and left deep holes with its fangs. She counted a dozen cave entrances, and the shadows cast from adjacent mountains likely hid dozens more. Her mouth dry, she heard Folke chuckle. Her reaction was as he predicted. She closed her eyes and sent a question to Hemming.

"Are you able to fly up to those mines and see if any of them are inhabited?"

"No child. A bird is not meant to be underground. I can fly past the entrances, but I doubt I will have much success," said the falcon.

"And if I command you to enter the mines?"

"You can try, but you forget I have a will of my own," he answered. *"Are you already making the same mistake as that arrogant Pan and thinking of me as a mindless object?"*

"I'm sorry Hemming. I'm desperate. It will take several lifetimes to search all those tunnels."

"Then you better calm your nerves and start using your head," he advised.

Freyja covered her eyes and spun away from Torsten and Folke. She didn't want either of them to see her tears.

"We had better get moving, little mouse," said Torsten. "The light fades."

Freyja was about to nod when she saw the tiny caravans and gypsy tents again. Hemming mentioning Pan triggered an idea in her head.

"We wait here," said Freyja.

Torsten looked at her. "Why?"

"I think I know how we can find the dwarves," she answered. "We make camp here, but don't pitch the tents and don't start a fire. We may need to move quickly."

"What are you thinking?"

"Trust me. Over there are some boulders we can use as shelter away from the wind." To her surprise, Folke obeyed the command and lumbered over to the large rocks, planting himself against one of them and lit his pipe. Torsten wanted more of an explanation but didn't want to waste energy arguing and instead said, "We eat a cold dinner then, but as the night settles, I will have a campfire set up just in case. We will not survive the night in this cold without one."

"I hope we will not have to stay out here all night, but we should rest as much as possible now," she said.

"If you plan to move around at night then we must use lanterns," said Torsten scanning the terrain.

"Agreed," said Freyja. She looked at Hemming, and before the question could be asked, the falcon ruffled its feathers.

"Yes, I can see very well at night and can help you avoid any rocky pitfalls," he said.

"Thank you," she whispered to the bird, scratching its breast with affection.

As the sun's amber rays issued one final farewell before disappearing below the horizon, Freyja huddled in her cloak and stared belligerently at the mountains. Torsten took the first shift to sleep and buried himself in blankets close to a boulder. Folke ate with them and then leaned back, closing his eyes before dozing off. He seemed immune to the chill, but Freyja retrieved his blanket anyway and covered him where he sat.

When Asmund and Asta appeared amongst the twinkling firmament, Freyja looked at the moons and sent a silent prayer to her brother, telling him to hold on. The twin moons inched their way closer together signalling the festival would soon be upon her. Unless a cure was administered to the sick children, she doubted the village would proceed with any celebration.

Beneath the weight of fatigue, Freyja closed her heavy eyelids and dozed. She dreamt her father was wandering the mountains and discovered a cave away from the blizzards. Entering, he notices a faint glow and walks over to discover a brisingr stone the size of his fist. Falling to his knees in exhaustion and joy, he picks up the stone but then feels the ground tremble. He turns to see the silhouette of Skadi the giant blocking the exit holding a torch the size of a small tree.

Freyja awoke with a scream calling out for her father. Disoriented and shivering, she stood on stiff legs and shook her feet to try and get some feeling back into them. Torsten was still asleep and Folke's snoring sounded loud enough to wake up creatures in hibernation. How long did she doze? She looked up, intending to gauge the night sky, but her eyes caught something else and a gasp escaped her lips.

Freyja raced over to her companions and shook them. With a trembling finger, numb even with gloves on, she pointed to the mountain.

"What am I looking at?" asked Torsten, rubbing his eyes.

"Th-there!" said Freyja through chattering teeth.

In daylight, they would not have seen it, but in the darkness of night, it was plain for all of them to see. Halfway up the side of the mountain, the unmistakable glow of light emitted from a cave entrance.

With a triumphant smile, Freyja proclaimed, "Like P-Pan said, dwarves need l-light in mines. In the name of Heimdallr, h-he who illuminates t-the world, there lies the c-candle to guide us."

Torsten turned to her grinning, and even Folke couldn't hide the twinkle in his eyes. Freyja had done it. She had found a mine still inhabited by dwarves.

Chapter 10

Dwarf Brothers Three

The trek up the side of the mountain was not as arduous as Freyja anticipated. One of the benefits of it being mined was that when the dwarves populated the area, they ensured proper paths and roads were built into the mountainside. This eased the transport of the treasures they unearthed.

With their lanterns lit and Hemming spying dangers from above, the group was able to progress toward the beacon of light emitting from the lone mineshaft. Hemming was especially useful as they lost sight of the cave light on several occasions around bends in the cliff face and avoided walking up paths that led away from their destination. While the guidance was welcome, this did not stop Hemming from informing Freyja that her sense of direction was terrible.

"No, not that way silly girl. You'll end up walking off a cliff."

"Turn around child! Can't you tell that road leads back down the mountain?"

"Do I need to guide your every step? Am I somehow speaking in riddles to deceive you like the trickster god, Loki? I said take the left path!"

The running commentary was merciless, and by the time they were near the entrance, Freyja was quite glad to send Hemming off.

"Are you sure I can't convince you to come into the mine?" she asked, not expecting him to change his mind.

"The sky is where I belong. I need to hunt for you have worked me to the bone," answered the falcon.

Freyja thought it was the other way around but did not respond. Instead, another question popped into her head. *"Hemming, how far can we communicate like this?"*

"Only in death can our connection be severed. If either one of us were to fall, the other would know," he said.

"That's a bit morbid but thanks for that." Freyja held out her gloved arm and let Hemming perch on it. *"So even if we cannot see each other, we will be able to talk like this?"*

"You raise an interesting question. As you are the first I have ever served as master, I do not know whether physical distance will limit our ability to

communicate," said Hemming, letting out a squawk.

"I guess we will soon find out."

As they approached the cave entrance, Freyja felt an unusual tug in her chest at the thought that Hemming would not be with her inside the mountain. Though their companionship had thus far been brief, she could not imagine being apart from the beautiful bird.

The entrance was wide, but only high enough for Folke to enter without bumping his head. The old man touched the ceiling with one hand, brushed the snow out of his beard with the other, and peered in with squinted eyes. Torches held in sconces lined the walls at even intervals down the tunnel. Two large iron braziers burned, both contained a healthy amount of coals, and Freyja guessed it was these flames they saw from their camp by the waterfall. For a mineshaft, the place was almost welcoming except for a wooden sign pitched in the middle of the entryway that said:

Unless you are one
of the Stonefist brothers three
You will be killed on sight
so turn around and flee!

Torsten unsheathed his sword and took the shield from his back and strapped it to his arm.

From behind, Folke grumbled, "I told you they were greedy creatures."

Freyja tried to discern what lay ahead, but the tunnel wound steeply down and soon curved around a corner out of sight. Not liking the idea of how deep they would have to go, she set one of the dials on her compass to the entrance of the mineshaft.

With a flutter of its wings, Hemming launched into the air away from the entrance but not before saying, *"Quaint message. I never knew dwarves could rhyme. Godspeed my child. I will be flying around out here and wait for you unless I sense the light of your life extinguished."*

"Thanks." Freyja sent the mocking thought out into the cold winter night. She followed Hemming's flight high into the skies and wondered whether the falcon was capable of understanding her sarcasm.

*   *   *

Freyja learned that all sense of time vanished when you were underground. Being able to see the sun and the moons was a luxury taken for granted. After an indeterminable period following the descent of the tunnel, she could not guess whether the dawn of a new day had arrived. Thank the gods that the tunnel did not branch off into multiple paths otherwise they would be lost. When they arrived at an underground cavern, and Torsten called for a halt, Freyja welcomed the respite.

The cavern's ceiling was high, but stalactites hung like frozen blades, making Freyja uneasy. The floor was smooth, and the walls were cut in a way that allowed for two doors to be built into the room. The one they walked through was set ajar, while an oaken door stood closed on the opposite side. Folke lumbered over, tested the handle and found it unlocked. "There are stone steps that lead down to another tunnel," he said.

"Then we stop here," said Torsten. "Little mouse, you sleep first. You didn't get to rest properly outside. I will keep first watch."

Freyja returned a weak smile, collapsed on her blankets and closed her eyes. Images of her father appeared again, this time shackled to a wall in a cave. She threw her arms around him only to discover that she was hugging her brother, who was lying chained to a bed, pale and weak. Through stinging eyes, she tugged at the restraints but could not release him. The sound of the rattling links taunted her as she cried out.

When she woke, the absence of sky gave no indication of how long she slept. A grogginess swam before her, and the sound of rattling chains echoed in the cavern causing confusion to ring in her head. She didn't realise she was no longer dreaming until the cold steel of a blade pressed against her throat.

Wide eyed and squirming backwards, Freyja found herself surrounded by three strangers. They were short with long braids of hair, neat beards, and large ears that stuck out from underneath helmets. Their arms and legs bulged with muscles like small granite boulders. Each wore thick boots, a leather tunic, and a bandolier strapped diagonally from one shoulder down to their opposite hip. The bandolier held a number of pockets, and items that dangled from it included a pick, lantern, waterskin, and hammer.

To Freyja, their stature and appearance would not have been imposing, if not for the fact that each held a shiny sword in a way that showed they were skilled with the weapon and were prepared to use it.

The three dwarves looked identical except for their helmets; each depicted a different symbol on its front. One had an eagle, another a dragon, and the third an ox. The dwarven helmets were polished to a healthy sheen, indicating they were a source of considerable pride.

"Intruders," said the dwarf with the eagle helmet.

"Interlopers," said the dwarf with the dragon helmet.

"Incisors," said the dwarf with the ox helmet.

Eagle helmet dwarf looked at ox helmet dwarf and said, "You idiot, incisors are teeth."

"Oh right," said ox helmet dwarf. "Um…"

"Try invaders," suggested dragon helmet dwarf.

"Ah thanks brother," said ox helmet dwarf. "Invaders!" he shouted.

Asserting control over the situation once more, eagle helmet dwarf pointed the tip of his sword at Freyja and said, "Your guards are a tad useless my lady. We thought the giant would cause us trouble, but he surrendered as soon as we took down the young one."

Freyja spun and saw both Torsten and Folke were gagged with metal cuffs bound around their ankles and wrists. Torsten fought against his chains to no avail, his face flushed from trying to scream over the handkerchief stuffed in his mouth. Not being able to protect Freyja caused him to boil over. Old man Folke sat still next to him and gave Freyja a small shrug in apology.

"We are not here to fight you," said Freyja.

"Then why does he have a sword and bow?" sneered eagle helmet dwarf pointing at Torsten.

"For protection," she explained. "Against bandits along the roads."

"I would say you're the bandits here," said eagle helmet dwarf. "Come to rob us of all our hard work. Yes, that's what you all are, bandits."

"Burglars," said dragon helmet dwarf.

"Bevellers!" shouted ox helmet dwarf.

"Idiot," said eagle helmet dwarf. "A beveller is a builder who smooths the edges of stone slabs. I don't want to hear you talking anymore."

Ox helmet dwarf looked downcast but perked up a little when dragon helmet dwarf leaned over and whispered, "Try brigand next time."

Eagle helmet dwarf rolled his eyes. "Do you deny you have come to rob us my lady? Who are you anyway?" he demanded, flashing his blade close to Freyja's face.

"My name is Freyja, and I do deny any intent to rob you," she replied. "My friends and I are here to do business with you. Nothing more. We seek a brisingr stone. Even one the size of a pebble will suffice. Had we known dwarves would greet us this way, we would never have bothered." She hoped her tone sounded aloof and did not contain any hint of the true desperation that bubbled inside her.

"A brisingr stone you say?" asked eagle helmet dwarf. Glancing sideways to his brothers, a devilish grin passed between them. They lowered their swords and bowed. "Apologies my lady. You have come to the right place. My name is Ardur Stonefist, and these are my younger brothers, Boltin and Cragor Stonefist. Please excuse Cragor, he's had one too many bumps on the head as a child." Cragor blushed beneath his ox helmet.

"I will accept your apologies if you release my friends," said Freyja.

"Of course," said Ardur as he waved to his brothers, who went over and unchained Torsten and Folke.

Torsten pulled the handkerchief from his mouth, rubbed his wrists as he walked over to Freyja and said, "They appeared through a secret entrance hidden in the side wall. I was watching the doors, and they were upon us before I could even raise my sword. Folke did nothing but submit to their mercy. I'm sorry."

"Nothing to apologise for," said Freyja as she touched his arm in reassurance. "And Folke has said before that he is no warrior, so do not be angry with him."

With her friends released, Ardur asked, "How will you pay for a brisingr stone my lady?"

Ever since her discussion with Pan, Freyja pondered two things. The first was how to find the dwarves, and the second was what to trade for a brisingr stone. She had little to offer, but any attempt was better than none. "I have a bit of gold," she replied.

"Show me," said Ardur. Freyja retrieved the small pouch, but before she could open it, the dwarf said, "That is not enough."

Freyja steeled herself. "I have this compass that my father gave me. It is magical," she said.

The three dwarves crowded around the device as she held it in her hand. Ardur let out a low whistle and said, "A fine device but still not enough."

"My father is a blacksmith," said Torsten. "I offer you any of my weapons."

"Not interested," said Ardur but raised a hand in thought. "Hold one moment. I need to discuss something with my brothers." They moved away and formed a tight circle, whispering to each other. When they returned, Ardur looked at Torsten and asked, "Are you learning from your father? You know how to work a forge?"

Torsten nodded and a ray of hope pierced the dark desperation in Freyja's chest.

"There is something that you could do for us. A trade of services so to speak. If you perform three tasks for us, you will have much more than just a brisingr stone by the end of it," said the dwarf. The torchlight reflected off his eagle helmet as he revealed a large smile from beneath his beard. "Do we have a deal?"

"What are the tasks?" asked Freyja, wary of the lack of detail.

"All in good time," said Ardur. "If you can't do the tasks then the deal is broken, and you can be on your way, but accomplish them, and your reward will be the stone you desire."

The thought of her brother chained to death was all that was required for Freyja to make her decision. "Okay, you have a deal," she said.

"Excellent," said Ardur. "You won't regret it. If all goes to plan you'll not only get a stone, but also a very pretty necklace."

Chapter 11

The First Task

The Stonefist brothers led Freyja down the steps and along a tunnel that appeared to go on for an eternity. Their torches cast shadows in all directions, causing her to become disorientated. She noted with some dismay that they passed several iron doors, which were all closed, and gave the impression she was in a series of dungeons. Her heart thumped, as if in its own prison cell, against her rib cage, and she tried not to think of torture chambers and laboratories where dark experiments were being conducted.

When Ardur halted at an iron door that looked to Freyja like all the others, she was surprised when it was revealed inside to be a very large and spacious smithy. Torsten couldn't disguise the awe on his face, for the workshop was impressive. Along the walls hung hammers, chisels, and tongs of various shapes and sizes. Anvils sat next to several forges situated in a semi-circle in the room, and hardy tools and fullers sat on work benches in easy reach for a blacksmith to work with hot metal. Next to each anvil sat a large rectangular slack tub, filled with water, and used to submerge hot metal when cooling.

"Welcome to the Astarite Forge," said Ardur, waving both his arms around the smithy. "This place was built by my ancestors during the time of war between Asgard and the Frost Giants, whom you call the Jotnar. It was here that dwarves of renown forged some of the greatest weapons Asgard has ever seen." He walked over to the centre forge, which was the largest of them all. "It was here that the star Astarite fell from the heavens, and its heart used to ignite this furnace. From its flames, it produced a metal never before seen on Asgard, and used to create Thor's mighty hammer, Mjolnir, and Odin's spear, Gungnir. The origins of enchanted Astarite came from here."

"Astarite," whispered Torsten. "The metal of legends."

"Indeed, young Asgardian," said Ardur. "Since the Frost Giants were banished to Jotunheim, and the war ended, this place has remained silent. No fire has burned within these ovens, no hammer has echoed throughout these tunnels, and no sparks have lit up the depths within these mountains for a millennium. Most of my kind left centuries ago, but my brothers and I have returned. We wish to reignite the forges and have our names written into history."

An excited chill ran down Freyja's spine. She stood within a unique part of Asgardian history, and if Torsten could assist in some way, they would be one step closer to securing a brisingr stone.

"The size of this forge requires many hands," said Torsten. "Is this the first task you were referring to? You need my help to work it?"

"We do, but this is not the first task," said Ardur. "Boltin will show you where the first task lies, while Cragor and I will remain here to prepare the smithy."

They followed Boltin along an arched hallway and entered a square room covered in polished marble slabs. In the centre sat a podium with a strange looking object perched on top of it. As soon as her foot touched the first slab, Freyja felt the weight of magic.

"My brothers and I have barely scratched the surface of the secrets held within these mountains," said Boltin. "Our ancestors recorded very little during the time of war, so the knowledge was lost from generation to generation. It is one of our failings that we desire strong ale and gemstones more than books." The dwarf walked over to a wall, and ran a rough hand over the marble. "I am sure you sense the dwarven magic in here. It covers every wall, floor, and ceiling. We stand inside a vault, or to be more precise, the door to a vault."

Freyja took off her winter clothes and shoved them in her pack. The dwarven magic was hot and heavy like molten lava. "A vault for what?" she asked hoarsely, her lungs burned as she watched Torsten and Folke also remove their heavy clothing.

"This much magic could only mean something valuable was held here," explained Boltin. "It represents a lock with a specific combination, and it took us a long time to figure out the first part." Leaning close to the wall, Boltin whispered a series of words in dwarvish. To her astonishment, Freyja saw letters appear on the marble slabs like watching an invisible quill write a message. It read:

Behind here lies the remnants of a star
Though it will appear like from afar
A pinpoint of light in the night skies
To hold it you will need your eyes
To locate the keyhole in the door
The pinpoint is the key to the core

"Remnants of a star," whispered Torsten. "Behind that wall lies Astarite?"

"We believe so," said Boltin. "Now come over to the podium." They moved to the centre, and Freyja saw that the strange square object on top of the podium had a glass eyehole. "Go on, take a look," urged the dwarf.

Freyja bent down and placed one eye in front of the eyehole while closing the other. "I can see the wall with the writing on it," she said. "But it's all tiny like the whole thing has shrunk."

"Yes, it's like looking at it from afar, right?" said Boltin.

"Just like what the writing says," pondered Freyja. "Is it magic that makes it tiny?"

"No, the eyeholes have curved lenses that make objects look further than they are," said the dwarf. "It's not magic but the walls are. This room is the door but we can't find a keyhole. We've searched every inch with no success. Ardur was so frustrated he tried to hammer the wall down, but the magic protects it and prevents anyone forcing their way to the Astarite. It is truly a dwarven vault."

"So even though the star is so close, it might as well be a pinpoint of light in the night sky," said Freyja, linking her thoughts to the cryptic message on the wall.

Boltin nodded. "We thought this podium was the key since this device atop it makes everything appear small. We've tried moving it, but like the walls, magic prevents it from being removed by force. Cragor shattered his pick axe trying to knock it over. The device does not move or spin so you can only look at the wall with the writing. It is like a torture device, knowing the treasure is there but making it appear beyond reach."

Torsten and Folke started running their hands over the wall searching for anything unusual. "I'm telling you not even Odin's eye could divine past that barrier, and I would wager Thor's hammer would merely bounce off it," said Boltin with a sigh.

Freyja stared at the writing on the wall and watched as it magically faded. Boltin repeated the dwarvish words he spoke earlier, and the writing reappeared. "What is the meaning of the words you speak?" she asked.

"It is a basic command spell. It translates to 'see what is unseen' in the common tongue," explained Boltin.

Freyja still felt hot and stuffy. Dwarven magic permeated the air, making it difficult to even breathe without inhaling heat. The dwarvish command, the writing on the wall, and the glass eyehole all spoke of using one's vision. She knew the answer was there but tantalisingly beyond her grasp, like trying to reach a cookie jar on the top shelf. It reminded her of Frey and when they were younger. Even without a ladder, he always found a way to climb up and steal those cookies. With a grin, he would say to her, "It's always a matter of perspective. If presented with a problem you can't solve, change your perspective, and a solution might present itself."

Freyja wiped the sweat from her brow. The room was an oven, and her brother's advice came to her like a cool, whispering breeze making her realise she needed to escape the heat. So long as she stood inside that dwarven vault, the haze would continue to cloud her mind. She stepped back into the arched hallway and left the door open. As soon as her feet were no longer touching marble, the intensity of the heat disappeared. Washed away from her to be replaced by the mountain's dark chill. She could see the podium, the magical writing, and Boltin watching Folke and Torsten as they continued to examine the walls. The oppressive fog lifted from Freyja's mind, and the scene became clear.

"Behind here lies the remnants of a star... to hold it you will need your eyes," mumbled Freyja to herself. "To locate the keyhole in the door... locate the keyhole..." Freyja wasn't sure whether it was her new perspective from outside the vault, or the removal of the magical heat, or a combination of both, but an idea struck her as she strode back to the podium.

Bending down, she looked at the block containing the glass eyehole. Pushing on the block, it did not move or swivel as Boltin had said. Holding her breath, she looked at the lens, placed a delicate finger against it and pushed. The lens moved. At the sound of metal scraping against stone, the others stopped what they were doing and looked at Freyja. Sticking a tongue out in concentration, she slid the lens metal tube out, and then turned the tube around before reinserting it back into the cubed device. The lens now sat in reverse. She looked through the eyehole once more, and as she predicted, the entire wall was now magnified. In fact, she could no longer see the writing but only a single marble slab. A smile appeared on her face. "Take a look," she said to Boltin.

Boltin did not need to bend over as the eyehole was the perfect height for a dwarf. "It's all too big now. You can't see the wall. What am I meant to be looking for?" he asked confused.

"Look at the middle of the tile," suggested Freyja.

"There's nothing th- ," said Boltin pausing mid-sentence. "Wait. I think I do see something. It looks like a dot."

"It's a hole," said Freyja. With great care, she traced the path from the podium to the tile that was the focus of the lens. The others followed, and they all crowded around the single marble slab. "There it is," she said, pointing a fingernail next to it.

"By Odin's beard," whispered Folke. "You would never know that was there unless you used the lens to magnify the tile."

"But it's just a tiny hole," said Boltin exasperated. "You couldn't fit anything in there except a – "

"Pin," said Freyja.

"The pinpoint is the key to the core," quoted Torsten amazed.

Freyja retrieved the needle she purchased from Pan in exchange for her hair. It took a very steady hand to align the point of the needle with the pin hole. As she inserted the needle, a click could be heard as its tip touched something inside. Pulling the needle out, she leapt back with the others as a grinding sound echoed from behind the wall. Stone on stone, the grinding grew louder as a line appeared down the middle of the wall, separating it into two stone doors that slid outwards.

"Not possible," said Boltin gobsmacked.

Folke let out a hearty chuckle. "There is an old Midgard saying that goes, 'It's like finding a needle in a haystack.'" said the old man. "This vault was the haystack and young Freyja found the needle."

"Little mouse, how did you know you could remove the lens?" asked Torsten.

"I didn't," she said. "It was a guess. I just tried to look at it from a different perspective."

Boltin looked at Freyja in adoration before walking through the now open wall. The rest followed, and they entered another room that would have been pitch black if not for a chest that had its lid open. From within, a glowing white light poured forth illuminating the darkness, and as they walked over and looked in, Freyja glimpsed for the first time, a little piece of heaven.

Chapter 12

The Second Task

Without ceremony, Boltin closed the lid to the wooden chest that contained the remnants of a fallen star. Holding it above his head, on top of his helmet, he rushed out of the marble tiled room while the others trailed behind. Freyja stared at the chest as it bobbed up and down in time to the dwarf's footsteps. She sensed a different type of magic, a cold, icy wave of energy that emanated from the chest itself. The contrast from the heavy, molten lava magic that oozed from the dwarven vault made Freyja curious.

Ardur's eyes were upon her when Boltin described her actions in unlocking the vault. Though she could not discern his thoughts, it was obvious she had become far more interesting to him. She wavered beneath that penetrating gaze and was thankful when Boltin opened the chest, causing Ardur to look away. She expected him to show the same sense of awe that she felt upon glimpsing the star, but instead he nodded with grim satisfaction.

"Torsten, go over to that storage room. You'll know what to do when you look inside. Folke you might want to help him," instructed Ardur. "Okay brothers, let us make history."

The three Stonefist brothers carried the open chest and tipped its contents into the centre forge. Upon being freed of its wooden confines, light burst forth from the Astarite shards illuminating the entire workshop. Explosive bursts of heat crashed over Freyja, and she understood now the magic imbued within the chest. It contained not only the star itself but also its fuel, preventing the Astarite from dying out. The magic of the chest had shielded the star from releasing its heat.

"Torsten! Folke! Quickly, the coals!" shouted Ardur.

From a side door, Torsten and old man Folke emerged pushing wheelbarrows filled with coal. Torsten pumped his young legs forward while Folke lumbered behind, taking long strides that covered the distance in fewer steps. When they each reached the forge, the wheelbarrow was emptied of its coal into the hearth, and a small pile formed over the Astarite shards. It did little to quench the heat erupting from the star. Without pause, Freyja watched her two companions push their empty wheelbarrows back to the stockpile just as the Stonefist brothers appeared pushing their own barrows, freshly filled. In this way, the small pile soon became a large mound of coals burying the Astarite shards.

"Hurry! We must close it!" yelled Ardur, pointing to two wheels that poked out from either side of the forge. With impressive precision, the Stonefist brothers moved to the right side while Torsten and Folke moved to the left. In relative unison, they spun their wheels, and Freyja watched as the opening to the forge shrunk. As stone ground on stone, she stood back and realised that the centre forge was built and sculpted into the shape of a dragon's maw. A construct of dwarven ingenuity, stone combined with metal gears as the top and bottom of the maw slowly closed. Freyja was spellbound as the dragon forge came to life. It was like watching a live dragon inhale air in preparation to expel fire. Steel teeth closed hiding the Astarite shards and coal inside.

"Boltin, Cragor, open the valves!" ordered Ardur. "Torsten, Folke, to the bellows!" The eldest dwarf walked over and stood next to Freyja, surveying the operation with his arms folded across his chest. He chuckled at the sight of Freyja's wide-eyed expression. "The dragon awakens," whispered Ardur.

Freyja's skin prickled, and her nerves tingled as she hugged herself tight. Fear and wonder mixed in a potent concoction causing her insides to swoon. Boltin and Cragor moved around from their wheel to several dials that they began turning. Metal pipes that stuck out from the dragon forge's head opened up, and a large chimney built into the rock ceiling was ready to engulf the smoke released from the pipes.

On the other side, Torsten and Folke positioned themselves behind a giant bellows. A large silver nozzle, attached to the device, pointed into a horizontal pipe connected to the forge. Freyja could see the leather flexible bag that would expand when Torsten and Folke lifted its handle to inflate it with air. It required at least two sets of hands as Torsten released the valve on the side of the bellows, and the pair set about blowing air into the forge. Freyja could only guess how heavy the wooden handle was, as sweat glistened on Torsten's forehead and Folke's breathing became laboured. She imagined that the height-challenged dwarves would have used ladders to work the instrument.

Two enormous, round windows made of clear crystal acted as the dragon forge's eyes and allowed Freyja to peer inside. When they started to glow, she knew the coals were intensely hot, and as Ardur predicted, it was like watching a dragon awaken from slumber.

Freyja rushed to her friends with waterskins when Ardur called a halt. "'Tis no laughing matter," gasped Folke as he gratefully accepted the water. "Were we not here to assist, Ardur would require more than his brothers to ignite this forge."

"Never did I think I would live to see such a smithy," said Torsten with a wide grin. "Part of me didn't think this place even existed. That it was pure myth. We have done well. Surely we are close to acquiring a brisingr stone."

Freyja attempted to keep her tone level; the look Ardur gave her before still lingered. "We need to keep our guard up," she said. Before she could elaborate, the Stonefist brothers appeared before them.

"Stupendous," said Ardur.

"Sensational!" cheered Boltin.

"Sickening!" said Cragor happily, his ox helmet nearly falling off his head in excitement.

Ardur shook his head but didn't reprimand his brother this time. The ignited dragon forge put him in good spirits.

"We were destined to meet," said Ardur with a flourishing wave of his hand. "You and your companions have far exceeded my expectations. Come with me, my lady." He took a step toward the workshop exit, and Freyja proceeded to follow with

Torsten and Folke close behind, but Ardur raised a hand. "No, you lads stay here, and keep the forge burning with my brothers."

Torsten was about to protest, but Freyja patted his arm and said, "I'll be okay." The blacksmith son was surprised by her reassurance. This was not the little mouse he knew. She was half surprised herself at the sudden display of confidence.

"Do not worry, young protector," added Ardur. "I will not keep her long."

The blacksmith son did not approve and stared down at him. "Do not tarry," he said. "It would be a tragedy if the light of Astarite that we have so diligently brought to flame should be doused."

The threat did not appear to phase the dwarf as he returned a wicked smile and led Freyja away. She glanced one last time at Torsten's worried expression before disappearing out the workshop and tried to remain composed. Ardur was almost skipping along the hallway, past the many identical doors she saw earlier, and whistled a tune that echoed eerily underground. Her imagination conjured up torture chambers and jail cells once more. With as much calm as she could muster, she sent out a thought.

"Hemming, can you hear me?"

Silence. She counted three beats of her heart and tried again.

"Hemming? Are you there?"

Silence. The falcon's voice, even the reprimanding one, would have been welcome, but the magical bird did not respond, and Freyja felt her mouth go dry. Their mental link appeared to have limits. Any attempt to call for help would never reach her winged companion, and the thought caused her palms to become clammy. The amount of earth above her head weighed with ominous intent. She squeezed her eyes tight and forced her breathing to slow as Ardur stopped before a door and opened it.

Freyja peered inside and saw it wasn't anything from her nightmares. The room was small and contained several iron chests sitting on shelves. A single candelabra sat on a wooden table near the entrance, and Ardur lit it with flint and steel retrieved from one of the pockets on his bandolier. Holding it aloft, he strode in, and as if knowing what each chest contained off by heart, the dwarf picked one that sat on a high shelf. Without hesitation, he pulled out a large iron key and unlocked the chest. Freyja saw it was filled with leather pouches, and Ardur waved her over to grab one. There was considerable weight with the pouch she picked.

"Go on, open it," said Ardur.

She obeyed and saw inside shiny fragments of metal. Even from the dim candlelight, the fragments gave off a lustre that spoke of beauty and expense. "I've never seen anything like this," she whispered.

Ardur laughed. "You hold the metal eorium. One of the rarest ores in all of Asgard. The only metal worthy enough to be placed in the heart of the Astarite forge, and I daresay the only metal I could ever imagine to be adorned around your neck my lady."

Freyja raised a hand to her throat, not sure what Ardur meant.

"Did I not say, if you accomplished my tasks, you would end up with a pretty necklace?" he asked.

Freyja nodded, not trusting her own voice. The glint in the dwarf's eye filled her with unease.

"You will get to witness the true magic of our craft," he explained. "We will weave a necklace of eorium never before seen in Asgard. One that will make all others pale in comparison. It will capture day and night, the sun and the stars, and all creatures will speak of its magnificence. My name and the names of my brothers will be written down in history for what we are about to create."

Freyja wasn't sure how to react so she opted for humble appreciation. "It sounds something worthy of the gods, but please understand that all I wish for is a brisingr stone."

"Nonsense," scoffed Ardur. "You did what my brother and I could not by unlocking the vault and bringing us the fallen star. Your friends admirably performed the second task of igniting the forge. All of that hard work cannot go to waste. The Stonefist brothers will become blacksmiths of legend!"

The fervour in the dwarf's eyes was plain for Freyja to see, so she didn't want to belabour her point and focused instead on the matters at hand. "I'm sure now the forge is lit, your efforts will rival your ancestors," she said. "But what of the third task? You have mentioned only two."

The wicked smile that Ardur flashed Torsten before returned along with the penetrating gaze he had given her when Boltin delivered the Astarite. "The third task is very simple, my lady," he said. "The greatest artefacts that my ancestors crafted for the likes of Odin and Thor could only unleash their full potential through the combination of two additional ingredients. Like all things, you can only ever reach your true worth through blood and sweat." He thumped his chest with a fist. "The dwarves provide the sweat. We thrive before the burning star." He then pointed a finger at her. "All you need to do is provide a drop of your blood."

Chapter 13

The Final Task

Upon explaining the final task to Torsten, Freyja was taken aback by her friend's reaction. "Absolutely not!" objected Torsten.

"Why?" she asked.

The blacksmith son glanced at the Stonefist brothers huddled together and watching them from a distance. He placed a hand on Freyja's back and guided her to a corner of the workshop. "Have you forgotten little mouse?" he whispered. "The tetanarium. You give one drop of your blood, and the infection will seize you. We both have been exposed to it in the village, and it is only the luck of the gods that you haven't had nary a scratch to your delicate body."

"But it is the only way to get the brisingr stone," said Freyja, somewhat alarmed that she forgot the threat of the tetanarium still hung over her.

Torsten asked Folke, "If she gives her blood and contracts the tetanarium, the three tasks are still complete, and we get the brisingr stone. Can you then cure her right away?"

Old man Folke looked grim. "The stone is a key ingredient. The most important ingredient no doubt, but there are other parts to the potion. I need my alchemy tools, which are all back at home," he explained. "From the moment a child hurts themselves, it takes roughly a day before the tetanarium overcomes them."

Freyja wanted to ask more questions, but their discussion was interrupted. "Shall we begin?" asked Ardur. His tone was level, but Freyja could see the impatience burn in his eyes. "A single drop of blood, my lady, is all that is required."

Torsten took a step forward. "You need Asgardian blood, right? Then take mine."

Ardur raised a curious shaggy eyebrow. His brothers stood behind him. Boltin's mouth was a thin, straight line of disapproval, and Cragor appeared worried. Freyja couldn't decipher what their expressions meant, but strangely it appeared they were aimed at their eldest brother. However, Ardur remained oblivious, his attention focused on Torsten.

"The necklace is designed for Freyja," explained Ardur. "It is the way of all dwarven blacksmiths that the magic infused is linked to its intended user. Thus, the need for their blood."

"But why choose Freyja and not I or old man Folke?" asked Torsten.

"We said from the beginning all we want is a brisingr stone. You do not need to make me a necklace," interrupted Freyja, surprised by her own audacity.

Ardur waved a finger, reprimanding her. "Then you renege on our deal. The necklace is part of the third task." He stood with an air of superiority. "I do not understand why a mere drop of blood is of concern, but if you do not wish to perform the third task then you can be on your way. Return to your village empty handed. It is not my loss."

Freyja saw again the look of discomfort on Ardur's younger brothers. Boltin frowned with his arms crossed, and Cragor stared at the ceiling as if not wanting to be part of the conversation. Some sort of friction had occurred between Ardur and his younger brothers, but the reason why eluded her. Regardless, whatever their disagreement, it was not going to change her current situation. Ardur held the upper hand. "One drop," she said.

"Freyja!" protested Torsten.

She looked at her friend and old man Folke. "We have a day," she whispered. "We get the stone and return to the village with all due haste. Torsten, if the tetanarium takes hold and I fall unconscious…"

"Then I will carry you," said the blacksmith son. "I will retrieve you from the depths of the underworld, Helheim, if I have to."

Freyja smiled her thanks before returning to Ardur. "Let us complete the third task," she said.

"Excellent," said Ardur, rubbing his hands. Signalling his brothers, they set about melting down the eorium, but not before Cragor gave Freyja one last sad look that flooded her with unease.

She wanted the comfort of Torsten to talk to, but he and Folke went back to helping the dwarves with the dragon forge. All she could do was sit back and watch the Stonefist brothers at their craft. They each donned thick leather aprons and gloves that hung off hooks against one of the walls. Ardur threw what she thought was a blanket at her. She caught it and saw it was actually a robe and surprisingly light given the thickness of the material.

"When the sound of molten metal being hammered on anvil echoed through this mountain, Asgardians and dwarves worked this forge," said Ardur. "But this smithy is like no other, so you'll be wanting to put that on."

Freyja did as she was told. Upon closer examination, she saw the leather robe was covered in layers of overlapping discs. The aprons and gloves the others wore also appeared to be made of the same material. "Dragon scales," said Ardur. He grinned. "When the Astarite forge breathes fire, it's the only thing that'll protect you."

Though the unease sat in the pit of her stomach, she couldn't help but be mesmerised. As the maw of the dragon forge opened, the smithy erupted with heat. Freyja imagined that this was what it would be like in the heart of a volcano. Even beneath her dragon scale robe, she could feel the heat but it was bearable. She didn't want to think what it would be like without it.

Ardur raised his arms in the air and let out raucous laughter as if seeking to embrace the giant forge like a loved one returning from a long journey. The flames reflected in his eyes as he gleefully placed several pieces of eorium metal into a stone bowl. Without warning, Boltin appeared at Freyja's side and said, "Your turn, my lady. If you will?"

Freyja swallowed the lump in her throat, retrieved her goblin sewing needle from its velvet pillow, and showed her hand. As gentle as he could, Boltin pricked her finger with the sharp pin before handing it back to her. A tiny bubble of crimson appeared on her fingertip as Boltin retrieved a small piece of eorium and watched the droplet fall on it.

He then put the piece in the stone bowl amongst the others.

Reaching over for a pair of long tongs sitting on a workbench, Ardur held the scissor-like device and picked up the bowl. As the dwarf approached the forge, arms extended, and placed the bowl into the fiery maw, it was like watching a child trying to feed a monstrous beast.

It didn't take long for the eorium to become liquid metal within the furnace of the Astarite star. Ardur poured the molten eorium into moulds while Boltin retrieved another piece of the metal and softened it amongst the hot coals.

Freyja wrapped a bandage around her finger. She felt disbelief that something so small could cause the tetanarium to infect her, but recalling the tiny cut her brother sustained caused her mouth to go dry. It was enough to make her close her eyes and prepare herself for the worst.

Not wanting the fear to overcome her, she focused on the final task, and it became apparent that making a necklace was quite different to forging a sword. Working with bits of metal in order to construct a piece of jewellery required delicate instruments like pin hammers, small chisels, clamps, brushes, and other tools she didn't recognise.

Much to her surprise, it was Cragor who assembled the necklace. As everyone else went about closing the maw of the dragon forge, Cragor was at a workbench taking the eorium out of their moulds and combining them with the soft, heated pieces that were hammered into different shapes. With a dexterity that belied his chubby fingers, Cragor formed a necklace of such stunning quality that it took Freyja's breath away. The eorium chain emitted a silver light as if it were alive, each link connected seamlessly into a dazzling array of metal lace the width of one of Freyja's fingers. Hanging off the chain was an eorium teardrop pendant infused with the light of the Astarite star, and it glowed in time with its mother chain. The surface of the pendant contained a hole, which she assumed was where you could insert a gemstone.

"It's beyond anything I could have possibly imagined," whispered Freyja. "It is like you captured a star and turned it into a necklace."

Cragor beamed with pride, his chest puffing out as he presented the necklace to Freyja.

"Extraordinary," said Freyja as she held the delicate chain in her hand.

"Exceptional," said Boltin.

"Excellent?" said Cragor tentatively. Boltin gave his younger brother a nod, and a pat on the back.

145

"Yes, my little brother does have a knack for trinkets. You come to me if you want a sword or spear made," said Ardur bemused. "Nevertheless, it is incomplete. The time has finally come for your reward. Follow me, my lady."

Before she left, Torsten asked, "How do you feel?"

"The same for now," she answered, showing her bandaged finger.

"Please assist my brothers in shutting down the forge," said Ardur. "We will be right back."

As they exited the workshop, Freyja marvelled at the necklace. "I can't believe this was made for me," she said.

"It is well deserved," said Ardur. "You have helped us unlock our history and have made it possible for the Stonefist brothers to forge a future in which all of Asgard will stand up and notice." He was walking very fast, but Freyja didn't notice as her eyes remained glued to the necklace. When they stopped, she saw they were at the end of the hallway, and a lone iron door stood before them. "This is where the brisingr stones are kept," he said with a bow. "After you, my lady."

The words sunk into Freyja's consciousness and resonated inside her chest. Her heart leapt as the distraction of the necklace was put aside. This was what she had been searching for, and finally it was within her grasp. She pushed open the door and walked in. It was very dark inside, but the glow from the necklace allowed her to illuminate the surroundings. Scanning the room, she frowned in confusion. "There's nothing in here," she said.

The sound of the door closed behind her. Freyja spun and saw the face of Ardur looking back through the barred window in the door. "When the brisingr stone littered the insides of this mountain, this is where my ancestors kept them," he said. "But when they departed, they took everything with them. I doubt there is even a pebble left, but you could always search the corners."

Freyja ran to the door, fear and panic crumbling her defences. It was locked. "You have betrayed me! We had a deal!" she shouted, banging on the door.

"I have shown you where we keep our brisingr stones, and I'm sure at the very least the dust of some of the stones still reside on that cold floor. So, I have kept my end of the deal, but I do not recall ever saying that after our exchange I would let you leave."

"You said we could be on our way," pleaded Freyja.

"Only if you proved useless and couldn't complete the tasks," said Ardur, removing his helmet and giving it a polish with a cloth. "But you not only completed the tasks, you proved to me what I suspected."

"Proved what?"

"That you're special," he replied, examining the shine off his eagle helmet.

"But there's nothing special about me." Freyja's tears bubbled to the surface.

"You are mistaken. The moment your blood ignited in the Astarite forge, I knew. It is through your blood that I will forge the greatest weapons ever seen in Asgard. Greater than Thor's hammer. Greater than Odin's spear. My name will become legend!" shouted Ardur.

Freyja cringed backwards, stumbling over her own feet, and falling to the floor. There was a madness in his eyes. A madness she should have seen before. As the sobs escaped her lips, and the dust of the empty storage room made her cough and splutter, she heard Ardur's laughter echo through the hallway as he walked away.

Chapter 14

Holding Hope

The stone floor was hard and icy. Everything seemed to slow down and freeze in place. Freyja stared unmoving at the glow of the eorium necklace that she held in her hand. The dirt and dust of the room covered her clothes, and she coughed every time her cries caused her to inhale. Old man Folke had been right. She should never have trusted those greedy dwarves.

The ramifications of Ardur's trap were too many. Their weight made her want to sink into the earth and disappear. She was now a prisoner inside a mountain where brisingr stones were a distant memory. A hope crushed into dust and as empty as the room she now resided in. The children of the village would not be saved, her brother could not be cured, and her own life wasted from shedding a single drop of blood. Torsten and Folke would be turned into slaves. The Stonefist brothers would blackmail them into doing their bidding under threat that they would kill her. Torsten would work tirelessly on the forge if it meant she was spared.

Not that the dwarves would be able to use her for long because of the tetanarium.

Freyja's sobs halted. *Wait, they don't know about the tetanarium.* The thought stuck as she stared through blurry eyes at the iron door that blocked her way. Like the links in her eorium chain coming together, the pieces of an idea gathered. A plan to escape.

She sat up and didn't realise how much she was caked in dirt. Beneath the necklace's faint glow, her hands were the complexion of the terracotta forest earth. If this room was once used to store brisingr stones, the only conclusion was the stones were of similar colour. The orange clay like texture reminded her of the water blossom pea tree, and another piece fell into place. The problem was the plan was dependent on convincing the dwarves she was infected. *Did they even know what tetanarium was?* If they didn't, she needed a backup plan.

The eorium necklace flowed in her hand like cool, liquid metal. Its beauty was a labour of blood and sweat, but there was something else. A critical component that Ardur was oblivious to, but she was acutely aware of. It shone in Cragor's eyes, the moment she complimented him on his creation. The necklace was also a labour of love. Freyja rose to her feet and started pacing the room. That explained the looks of disapproval and discomfort from Boltin and the youngest brother. That was the friction she observed. They did not approve of what Ardur was doing. If she was right, her backup plan was now formed.

As if confirming her suspicions, Boltin appeared at the barred window. "My lady, I have some food for you." He was initially impassive, but a frown appeared when he saw how dishevelled she looked.

"I need to speak to Ardur," she said.

Boltin hesitated. Conflict strewn across his face. "Ardur ordered me to bring you this food. That is all."

"And you have done that. I simply request to speak to him." She held the necklace up to the window. "Please Boltin. If he wishes to use my blood for more creations, he'll want to know what I have to say, and you should bring the others as well, especially Folke."

"I will see what I can do," he replied and handed her some dried beef, cheese, and bread through the window.

As he headed back up the hallway, she added, "Please bring my pack also!"

Boltin gave no indication that he heard as she slumped down against the door and nibbled at the cheese. The food brought back some sense of herself as the plans repeated themselves in her mind. She imagined Torsten standing over her, smiling as she sat huddled against the chill, a little mouse with her cube of cheese.

"I hope this works," she said to the illusion of her friend. She ate as much as her stomach would allow. The nervousness made it hard to keep the food down. At the sound of footsteps, she stood and saw the Stonefist brothers approach. Much to her chagrin, her friends were not with them, but at least, Boltin was carrying her pack.

"Your friends are unharmed," said Ardur anticipating her concern. "Young Torsten was so enraptured in helping us with the forge that he carelessly left his weapons in a neat bundle for us to take. Both he and the old man are chained up so they don't accidentally try to wander off. So, speak my lady, it has been a long day, and my brothers and I wish to sleep."

Freyja wasted no time. "Have you ever heard of tetanarium?"

"What is that? A metal?" asked Ardur.

"No, it's a rare disease that affects young Asgardians," she said. The dwarves not knowing the disease made things more difficult, but she wanted to make an attempt before using her backup plan. "My village has become infected with it. We have journeyed here to acquire a brisingr stone because it is a key component in the cure."

"I have never heard of the stone being used in such a way."

"Ask Folke, he is our medicine man. That's why I wanted you to bring him. He will be able to tell you."

"You bore me, my lady." Ardur yawned and scratched his behind. "Even if it is true. It is not my concern."

Freyja grabbed the bars on the window. "But it is your concern. All that is required to contract tetanarium is to sustain a cut." She raised her bandaged finger.

Ardur's eyes widened but then he laughed. "You're very clever my lady. Coming up with such an elaborate tale," he said. "Shame on me that you almost had me fooled. Such a perfect set of circumstances would make keeping you here a useless endeavour."

"You are blind to the truth, Ardur. Within one day I will come down with a fever, my body will experience painful spasms, and my mind will fall into delirium," said Freyja. "My infected blood will be useless, and it will be too late. Folke has the knowledge to stop it. You will need to free him, and help him if you wish to continue using my blood. I am not speaking with the tongue of Loki. I am not seeking to deceive you."

For the first time, Ardur didn't appear so sure of himself. Her conviction stirred a seed of doubt. "Even if what you say is true, you still need a brisingr stone, and I did not lie before. You stand in the place where those stones were kept."

"Then I shall die," she responded. "And if I die then allow me to do so at home with my family. I am no longer any use to you."

Boltin and Cragor remained silent, but their sympathy was apparent on their faces, and her words moved them. On the other hand, Ardur shook his head. "I have never heard of tetanarium. Everything you have said is a ruse to free you and your companions."

Freyja felt her hopes diminish. Her plan required Ardur believe in the threat of the disease, but he dismissed it. She fell on her backup plan and prayed for the best. "You will know I have spoken the truth within a day. It would be wise that you or one of your brothers stay and keep watch over me," she suggested. "Each hour that passes will be time lost."

Ardur looked at his brothers, not wishing to concede but knowing there was no harm in her request. "Cragor, you keep watch first, and we will rotate through the night," he grunted.

"Can I have my pack please?" asked Freyja looking at Boltin.

"Wait," interjected Ardur. "Give me that." The eldest dwarf emptied the contents of the backpack on the ground. He took her rope, flint, tinder, torches, and a small spade. Anything that could be used to escape, he confiscated.

"I was just after my waterskin," said Freyja. "The dust in this room has made my throat dry, and your brother didn't bring me any water with the food."

Ardur picked up her waterskin, unscrewed the cap and smelt inside.

"It's only water," she said. "You all look thirsty. Pour yourselves a cup if you don't believe me."

Boltin added, "We don't want her dying of thirst brother."

"I wouldn't mind having a cup," said Cragor. "It has been a hard day."

"Very well," said Ardur. His brothers retrieved a tin cup each from their bandoliers, and Ardur poured water into each of them. He then pulled out his own cup, filled it with liquid and handed it to Freyja while he held on to the waterskin. He raised it up in front of them and toasted to their future success. "May our names resound through Asgard and be etched into the hearts of our ancestors. The

Astarite Forge lives again, and we will create treasures this land has never seen. To the Stonefist brothers!"

Boltin and Cragor cheered, and Freyja lifted her cup also. As the dwarves quenched their thirst, Freyja made sure her cup went to her mouth but that the liquid did not touch her lips. "Ardur, come closer," she said, waving a delicate hand while she put her cup on the floor. "You haven't seen me with the necklace on."

Ardur walked to the barred window and peered in. His eyes looked a little glazed. "The necklace does your beauty justice, child. You have no idea how precious the blood is that runs through your veins."

Freyja raised her hands and put the delicate eorium chain around her neck. It felt cool against her skin and glowed a soft, silver light.

"It truly is meant for you. It is magnificent…" Ardur's words trailed off as he slumped against the iron door. Freyja shot out her hand through the window to catch him by the arm. The dwarf was snoring with reckless abandon.

"Marvellous…" said Boltin as he crumpled to the floor in slumber.

"Magical…" said Cragor as he crawled up into a foetal position and went to sleep.

Holding Ardur under one arm, she reached out with her other hand and took the ring of keys from his belt. Awkwardly, she managed to fit the right key and unlock the door from the outside. Freyja thanked Odin that dwarven doors were small, thus allowing her the ability to reach down far enough to find the keyhole.

She pushed the door open, sliding Ardur's limp form out of the way. "The stream from the water blossom pea tree is magical," she said, leaning over Cragor and kissing him on the forehead. "I'll have to thank Torsten for filling up our skins with it." She bent over and also gave Boltin a kiss on the cheek causing the dwarf to smile in his sleep.

Freyja rose, brushed the dirt off her clothes as best she could, and gave one last look at Ardur before kicking him in the leg. "I can't believe you're related," she said, before running up the hallway to free her friends from their chains.

Chapter 15

Unfulfilled Wishes

Like a dancing firefly, Freyja sped along in the darkness beneath the mountain, leaving trails of silver light from her necklace. Her pulse raced as she wondered how long the sleeping draught would last. The clinking of keys in her hand accompanied the echo of her boots as she poured her remaining energies into running. When she burst through the door of the smithy, it caused Torsten and Folke to look up startled. Both had cuffs on their arms and legs, and a long chain tied them to the wall where they crouched.

"How did you escape?" asked Torsten astounded.

"The waters from the blossom pea tree," she answered, flipping through Ardur's ring of keys and picking one she guessed would unlock their chains. "I kept one of the skins you filled with it." The key didn't fit, so Freyja began trying each one in turn. "My initial plan was to convince them that I had contracted tetanarium, so it was useless to keep me prisoner. I doubt my infected blood could be used in the forge. Unfortunately, they didn't even know what tetanarium was, so they believed I concocted the idea in order to be freed.

"When that didn't work, I had to persuade them to drink from the skin. Thanks to Ardur's suspicious nature and their own thirst from working the forge, it didn't take long for the waters to take effect." Halfway through the keyring, Freyja found a small iron key that fit and turned with a click, unlocking the chains.

Folke stood with a groan like a tree stretching its limbs. "The brisingr stone?"

"None. Ardur knew all along they didn't have any."

"Then there is nothing left to keep us here." He looked at Torsten. "Any idea how to get out of this rabbit warren?"

"Vaguely," answered the blacksmith son. "I am impressed that the dwarves are able to move through these tunnels without signs."

Freyja looked around the smithy; thoughts of escape were confined to the empty storage room and freeing her friends. Her nerves were on edge. Now that those goals were accomplished, she was unprepared to confront the maze of tunnels that they needed to traverse to get out of the mine.

The dragon forge lay silent, its eyes dark, and the fire within its belly extinguished. For a fleeting moment Freyja wondered whether she would end up the same, buried beneath the mountain, and the light of her life snuffed out like a blown candle flame. With the furnace heat gone, an ache sunk into her bones, and she put on her cloak to ward off the chill.

An object pressed against her chest pocket, and reaching in, she pulled out her compass. Her eyes widened. She *had* thought ahead. Rubbing dust off its surface, she peered at the dial set to the entry of the mineshaft. The arrow pointed west. Torsten saw what she was holding and clapped his hands with glee. "Little mouse, you are constantly full of surprises," he said, donning his pack. "I miss the sun. Let's get out of here."

* * *

The combination of the compass and Torsten's memory allowed them to return to the cavern where stalactites hung from the ceiling. From there it was only a matter of following the single long tunnel back up to the entrance. As soon as Freyja stepped over the threshold, the dawn of a new day greeted her, and tears of relief blurred her eyes. The terracotta forest was ablaze like a sea of golden foil as winds sought to carry the leaves away from tree branches.

"The mountain did not swallow you," said Hemming, the falcon's voice echoed in Freyja's mind. *"Have you acquired the stone?"*

"Hello to you too Hemming." Freyja rubbed the tears from her face. *"No, we have failed."*

The falcon glided in a wide arc, passing in front of the rising sun, before landing on Freyja's extended arm. *"A shame, so what now?"*

"We return to the village with all due haste. Please guide us down this mountain and through the forest."

"Very well child."

As they started their trek back home, Freyja's thoughts turned to her brother and the other children of the village. The momentary elation of seeing daylight was replaced now by trepidation, and as much as she tried to ignore it, her bandaged finger began to throb.

*   *   *

When nightfall arrived, they were back in the heart of the Terracotta Forest. Hemming had guided them to a grassy bank where they could camp by the west river. An impressive distance was covered thanks to the falcon's directions.

Freyja sat on her sleeping mat staring at the skies, and waited for the moons to appear. How close were Asmund and Asta now? Was the moon festival upon them? All sense of time evaporated inside that mountain, so how many days had passed was unclear.

Forcing her aching legs into motion, Freyja's gaze alternated between sky and ground, counting stars and collecting wood. By the time Torsten returned from the river with fresh water, she had a camp fire going.

"Where's Folke?" he asked.

Freyja looked around and saw the old man was absent. She shrugged, not at all surprised by Folke's disappearing act. "Looks like he's wandered off again. Probably pretending he was never involved in our attempt to get the brisingr stone. I doubt he wishes to face the wrath of my mother when we get home."

"Or my father," added Torsten. "I'll be cleaning the smithy slack tubs for the rest of the year." They both gave a half-hearted laugh. A feeble attempt to mask the fact that their quest to bring home a cure was a failure. The thought was prevalent in both their expressions, and Freyja watched as Torsten rose and retrieved an axe from his backpack.

"What are you doing?" asked Freyja.

The blacksmith son walked over to a tree and inspected its branches. Testing some of the thinner ones, he proceeded to cut down two slender poles the same length. He brought them over and laid them on the ground. "I'm building a stretcher," he said. "The tetanarium will take hold of you soon, and this will make it easier to transport you. As delicate as you are little mouse, I will not get far carrying your unconscious form on my shoulders."

Freyja swallowed the words stuck in her throat as she admired her friend's forethought. Torsten used one of his woollen blankets and wrapped it around the two poles.

"It would be easier if Folke was here to carry the other end, but I will drag you on this stretcher if I must. I swear to you I will get you home." He picked up the two poles and walked around with it behind him. The other end dragged along the ground, but the stretcher stayed together. Satisfied that it would do the job, Torsten put it back down and slumped next to Freyja. He placed a hand on her forehead and asked, "How do you feel?"

"My body aches, but I think that's from exhaustion," she replied, flushing at his touch.

"You feel warm," he replied, revealing a worried frown.

Freyja tried to control her blushing but failed and was thankful that the campfire did not illuminate her face much. She removed his hand and held it a moment. "I'm sorry I put you through all this Torsten," she said. "I'm sorry I let you down. Let everyone down. My brother…"

"Hush." Torsten embraced her. It was enough to squeeze out her tears, and she cried into his arms. "We had to try," he said. "Do not lose hope, little mouse. While we did not succeed, perhaps your father has, and he is already back in the village with a bag full of brisingr stones."

Freyja continued to cry, but the words sunk in. She had forgotten about her father and felt shame well up inside her. There was still hope even if it was slim. Torsten lay her down, and she looked up at the night sky. Asmund and Asta had begun their own embrace, their light finally started to overlap, and Freyja knew that the moon festival was only a day away. Torsten rummaged through his bag for some rations, and Freyja picked up her own pack and trundled down to the river.

"I need to wash off the mountain grime," she said.

"Don't be long," he replied. "I'll have sausages sizzling on a pan."

As she reached the water, Freyja spied a curtain of tall reeds and proceeded to undress. Stepping into the gentle current, she paused to admire the reflected starlight like pixie dust sparkling amongst the rippling reflections of the two moons. The waters were cold, having flowed down from the snowy peaks of the mountains, but she didn't mind because her body felt overheated. The hypnotic dance of the stream made her sleepy, and she sank into the river with delight. Her feet slipped over mossy stones as her body lay in an eddy pool. The dirt being washed away made her feel better. Finding a purchase against a rock, she planted her feet and lay on her back against the current. Her hair flowed like strands of seaweed as she stared up at the constellations, all of her head submerged except for her face peeking above the water.

Breathing deeply, Freyja felt her consciousness wane. Her body floated making it easy for her to release the exertions of the day. Her mind let go of how close she came to finding a brisingr stone. She had done what she could, and now there was a strong desire to let the current take her like a piece of jetsam to be washed away into the sea.

A silent wish for forgiveness was sent out into the night, hoping for it to reach her brother, Frey. Holding her breath, she closed her eyes and sunk into the river. The watery realm muffled the night time sounds, and all Freyja could hear was the slow beating of her heart. She wanted to remain there, and allow fatigue to draw her further into the abyss. Eventually her lungs protested, and she broke the surface to gulp in air. It left her dizzy as she dragged her sore body back to the bank.

Out of the water, a breeze caused gooseflesh to erupt over her skin and her teeth chattered. Drying as fast as her hands would allow, she realised her head was still spinning. Putting on some clean breeches, she lost her balance and fell to the ground. The impact causing pain to reverberate through her aching muscles. Struggling to put on the rest of her clothing, Freyja felt her chest constrict, and her palms go clammy.

By the light of the moons, she looked at her finger. The bandage had come off in the river. She tried to focus on where Boltin had pricked it, but instead several images of her hand blurred across her vision. Somehow, she managed to shove her dirty clothes into her bag and rose to her feet swaying with hair still dripping.

"T-Torsten." Her voice sounded small and weak. Taking a step, her knees buckled and her bag dropped from her shoulder. She felt hot again, perspiration stinging her eyes. It was as if she was back in the magical dwarven vault, and her lungs were being filled with lava. Her finger felt stiff. She also couldn't move her wrist, the joint seized shut. Through blurry vision, her skin appeared to start flaking and turn reddish brown like she was rusting all over. It was painful to lift her head. The back of her neck stiffened as if a hot poker was stabbing her. Falling forward, she managed to send out one final thought. *"Hemming, help me."*

As her face hit the ground and the darkness of night engulfed her, the last sound she heard was the shrill cry of a falcon.

Chapter 16

Star and Sun

Freyja shifted her weight and felt the comfort of a pillow behind her head. It was a strange sensation as her body protested. The movement didn't cause spasms of pain, which was what she expected. Instead it was merely the dull ache of limbs that still needed rest. Her eyes remained closed as she felt her chest rise and fall in steady rhythm. The searing heat that penetrated her lungs before was now gone. She tried to remember what happened after collapsing on the riverbank but failed.

With a small swallow, she attempted to flex her finger. The stiffness dissipated, and she turned her wrist and felt the soft folds of a blanket. This must be a dream, she thought. Or maybe she was in Valhalla where the dead reside. Carried off on the wings of a Valkyrie and delivered to the afterlife to celebrate in Odin's majestic halls until the end of days. But only the bravest are chosen, and she wasn't sure whether her unsuccessful quest would count.

She was afraid to open her eyes. The tetanarium had taken over, she was certain of this, and yet the fever and vertigo appeared to have left her. When the smell of pastry, cinnamon and tinkleberries caught her attention, she pictured the never-ending banquet in the halls of Valhalla. A table weighed down by the food of gods. She just never thought cinnamon and tinkleberry pie would be one of the delectable delights. The scent enveloped her like a comforting hug. It was the same smells that reminded her of her mother's kitchen. A treat that would greet her after working in the orchards all day. The memory made her eyes well up, and her stomach grumbled.

She let out a moan and felt the touch of a hand on her arm. "I kept my promise," said the familiar voice.

Freyja blinked and Torsten came into focus. His head was bowed, eyes closed as if he was in prayer. The late afternoon sun peeked through a window. He looked older, more lines on his face. Did she do that to him? The remorse made her bottom lip quiver, as she sought to contain her cries. In the end, she dragged him on a quest of futility and still he cared for her. There were shadows under his eyes. How much time passed? He was still holding onto her arm, so she lifted it to get his attention.

"Freyja!" Torsten's look of disbelief was mixed with confusion. "How can you be awake? How do you feel?"

She spied a pitcher of water on a bedside table. Her bedside table. Torsten saw what she was looking at, poured a glass and lifted her head so she could sip. The liquid soothed her throat. "I'm home?" she croaked.

"In your own bed," said Torsten with a wane smile.

"How did you – "

"A whole day's march along the west river with frequent breaks. You're not as light as you look even on a stretcher."

"Folke?"

"No idea. Probably back in his stone hovel with those strange plants and experiments. My father was the first to see us appear on the rise of the hill. He ran at us like a raging bull, and I feared that it would be safer to turn back to the forest. However, it was not his wrath but worry that greeted us. He carried you in his arms with me on his back the rest of the way. He had plenty to say, but his primary concern was whether we were okay. He took us straight to your house. I don't think I've ever seen your mother cry so hard."

175

"Mother," whispered Freyja, a soft cry that was barely audible. Yet as if by magic, a connection only a mother and her child could have, the bedroom door opened, and there stood Freyja's mother.

Upon seeing her daughter awake, Nerthus rushed over, placing a plate with a sliced tinkleberry pie on Torsten's lap and then engulfing Freyja to her bosom. She often smelt of flour and daffodils because if she wasn't baking in the kitchen, she was out in her garden. Their happy sobs mingled together as Torsten rose from his chair to give them some privacy. He stood by the window, looking out, and savoured the taste of the tinkleberry pie with an expression of pure bliss.

"How is this possible?" asked Nerthus, holding her daughter at arm's length.

"I do not know mother."

"It's a miracle. Odin must have heard my prayers and known I could not bear losing two children."

Freyja stiffened. "My brother, I have to see him."

"You can't my love. He is but a shadow." Nerthus shuddered as she put on a brave face. "It will not be long now."

Freyja shook her head, denying the finality of her mother's words. Her hair brushed her shoulder from a gentle breeze, nudging her into motion. With a resolve that surprised her mother, she slid her legs off the side of the bed and stood up.

Torsten put down his pie on the window sill but did not move. He recognised this newfound strength and restrained his first instinct to assist her. Freyja felt the familiar wooden floorboards beneath her bare feet. Two steps forward toward her door and that particular floorboard would squeak. Another four steps and the floor would dip slightly. Opening the door and turning right, it would be eight more steps to her brother's bedroom.

She kept her eyes on her feet, remembering a time when they were smaller and carefree. A time when it would require many more smaller steps to reach Frey's room and jump on his bed to wake him up. When she reached his door, she paused, and recalled those many days before how she stood afraid of what lay behind it. Now her insides weren't in knots. There was no bubbling of desperation. A calm and inner poise formed like a well inside her, and she could now draw from it.

As she walked in, everything around Frey's room was as it should be. A wooden bracket on the wall opposite his bed displayed his collection of weapons; an Asgardian yew bow gifted by their father, a heavy oblong shield with a deer emblazoned on its front, and a fine long sword with

a deerskin leather grip, both constructed by
Gudbrand the blacksmith. A trident and net also
hung on the wall. Frey used these not for fighting
but for fishing with their father. In one corner was a
tall wardrobe that contained the clothes that Frey
owned. A paltry number compared to her own.

In another corner was a desk and chair with a
low bookshelf that contained nine red leather-bound
tomes, each dedicated to the study of one of the
nine homeworlds. While Freyja was partial to
reading about Midgard, her brother preferred the
pages that spoke of Alfheim, the home of the Light
Elves. She had attempted on many occasions to
convince him, when they were older, to travel to
Midgard. Her brother would shrug, and ask her why
journey there when they could venture to a world of
creatures that were fairer than the sun and where
fairies flew through forests.

Above his desk, a framed illustration of the nine
worlds connected by the sacred ash tree, Yggdrasil,
hung by wire over a nail. Her brother would stare at
it for hours, memorising how the cosmos was
connected.

When she was little, she couldn't understand his
fascination with exploration. Their village provided
everything they needed, so testing the dangers
beyond the walls seemed foolish. It took significant

cajoling, and the promise he would remain by her side to venture even to the top of the hill. Only then did her eyes begin to open to the other marvels of Asgard.

Having traversed the Terracotta Forest and visited the gypsies, she now understood that these experiences brought enlightenment. Even the confines and trials of the mountain had made her grow, more so in terms of forcing her to draw on strength that was previously untapped. How Freyja wanted to share her adventures with Frey and tell him of the lessons learned. How she wanted to tell him that he was right. That the world, while filled with thorns, was also filled with roses, and life was meant to experience both. It also taught her that it was foolish to think that she could remain safe within the village. The tetanarium had taught her that.

Turning away from the picture of the world tree, Freyja approached her brother. She knew that even unconscious, her mother was still bathing him. The scent of lavender soap indicated his sweat was washed away every day. Frey was no longer tossing and turning from feverish nightmares, and the wracking pain had stopped eating away at his body. All that remained now was the still, gaunt form of her twin brother. A form she still recognised even if all his vitality had been stolen away by the disease. His breathing was now a shallow wheeze, the only indication he was still alive. Freyja knew he was holding on by the thinnest thread.

Biting her lower lip in a vain attempt to remain strong, bitterness and anger washed over her. She lay down next to him, squeezing herself on the edge of the bed and moving his frail arm behind her neck. His entire body remained limp, everything shut down except the bits of air he inhaled and exhaled. She caressed his sallow cheek hoping for a reaction. It was like the essence of him had seeped out, and all that was left was a shell.

Freyja thought there were no more tears to shed, but her eyes stung from some well not yet drained. Through the open bedroom window, the sun touched the horizon sending rays of amber light. Tonight, Asmund and Asta would become one, and the moon festival was meant to bring the village to life. Instead, she doubted any celebration would occur. The fathers and mothers would remain with their sick children. The snow-covered village would remain silent.

As the sunset rays reached into Frey's room, they splashed over Freyja's face as the flood inside her was released. She didn't notice the light touch the links of her necklace or the way the eorium began to glow. The teardrop pendant shone silver like a tiny Astarite star. As the tears ran trails down her cheeks, Freyja buried her face in the crook of her brother's neck. Her cries filled the room as a tear fell like a drop of amber onto the necklace. Working its way along the river of silver, it found a home in the dimple of the teardrop pendant. There it stopped and began to crystallize, forming a tiny stone.

Wiping her eyes, Freyja noticed the pulse of light coming from her necklace. Silver and amber mixed together, star and sun, night and day. Unbelieving she sat up and held the pendant in her palm. From the stone, a droplet of molten amber oozed out and fell on her brother's face, next to his nose. There it trickled into his mouth. Then, before her very eyes, Frey – beloved son of Njord and Nerthus, twin brother of Freyja – began to stir.

Chapter 17

The Brisingamen Necklace

Old man Folke pried open Freyja's eye with a thick thumb and finger. For someone who spent most of his life handling rocks, plants, and dirt, she was surprised at how gentle he was in his examination. He peered in both eyes for some time before asking her to open her mouth. Pressing a wooden spatula on her tongue, he shone a light down her throat, using a device that Freyja had never seen before. It reminded her of the looking glass in the dwarven vault except this one used a crystal that emitted a white light of its own accord. She sensed a faint magic within the crystal.

"Shouldn't you be more concerned about my brother?" The question was difficult to ask with her mouth open.

Folke didn't answer. Moments before, Freyja had called out to her mother when Frey regained consciousness. Nerthus and Torsten halted at the door in shock when they saw Freyja cradling her brother's head in her lap, and he was awake. When it registered what they saw, Torsten ran off to get Folke. The lumbering and measured gait of the old man must have received a jolt of lightning from Thor's hammer because he arrived shortly thereafter out of breath.

After Freyja explained, as best she could, the events leading up to her brother's awakening, she watched as Folke measured his pulse and listened to his breathing. He asked Frey if he was hungry, and when her brother nodded weakly, Folke asked Nerthus to prepare some soup.

"Nothing solid," he said before turning his attention to Freyja. He picked her up by the shoulders like a small box and planted her on a stool, much to her surprise.

Mumbling under his breath, Folke proceeded to poke, pry, and measure Freyja's physical faculties. She allowed the old man to examine her for twice as long as her brother. When he tapped her knee with a rubber mallet, causing her leg to kick out involuntarily, she lost her patience. "Enough, what has happened to me?"

Folke crossed his huge arms across his barrel chest and frowned behind square rimmed glasses. Still ignoring her questions, he reached out and held the eorium necklace in his palm. The necklace that now had a small, orange stone within its teardrop pendant, glowed like a miniature sun. When he finally spoke, it caused her to frown in return.

"Brisingamen." The word rumbled out of his throat.

"What is that? My necklace?" Freyja looked at her jewellery. With a gemstone in place, its startling beauty was complete.

"Yes, *brisinga* is another word for *brisingr* stone and *men* means necklace or torc," he answered. "My wee child, you are now the owner of the Brisingamen."

Freyja looked at the old man. She felt his proclamation was meant to mean something, but she didn't know what. "Just tell me whether my brother and I are going to be okay?"

For the first time since Freyja dared to walk into the old man's home and seen his excitement over a bunch of Midgard herbs, Folke responded with a genuine smile.

*   *   *

For the rest of that night, Freyja visited every sick child in the village with Folke. As if by desire, and the silent breaking of her heart at the sight of each bedridden youngster, the Brisingamen necklace shed a molten tear that once ingested revived the child. Little Eerika's parents called it a miracle. Calder the miller was in near hysterics when his sons, Birger and Brant, awoke bleary eyed. Even Einar, the first to collapse while tending the fields, was able to be cured.

The moons, Asta and Asmund, would be together for one week, which was how long the festival was meant to run. It took four days for the villagers to organise the food, stalls, tables, and wood for the bonfires, but no one cared about the missed time. It allowed not only for the festival preparations, but also for Frey and the other young Asgardians to heal and regain some strength.

On the fifth night, the celebrations begun. Tables were laden with food; roasted boar, pots of chicken broth, sizzling sausages, platters of fruit and cheeses, and kegs of ale and cider. Bards played their mandolins, piccolos, dulcimers, and kettle drums as music filled the winter air. The stalls opened and sold trinkets, wind chimes, crystal baubles, and packets of rock sweets. Life and joy returned to the village.

Freyja found she couldn't walk anywhere without being mobbed. Parents wanted to give food, and children wanted to hug her or take a peek at her necklace. The attention was overwhelming, and it didn't help that Frey encouraged the behaviour. He seemed to be getting enormous satisfaction that, for once, he was in her shadow instead of the other way around. It took a look of complete desperation before he rescued her from Calder the miller, who sought to add two large bags of flour to all the food she was already carrying. They managed to transport all their goods back home, and Frey suggested they go for a walk instead of returning to the festivities.

They exited the gates and made their way through the snowdrift. The sounds of singing, clapping, and chatter from the village faded away as the twin siblings made deep footprints side by side up the slope. Frey stopped often to catch his breath. It would take time before he would return to full strength, and Freyja offered to carry him on her back.

He laughed. "This cannot be happening. Who are you and what have you done to my sister? She would never offer to piggyback me. Especially when it is normally I who end up being the mule."

Freyja kicked white powder in his direction but knew he was right. When the snow was deep, as it was tonight, she would have asked to ride on his back in the past. She would doze while listening to him tell a story about the Light Elves or sing an old lullaby. Looking at him, the thick, woollen clothing couldn't hide the still gaunt frame underneath. His cheeks were too hollow and lips too thin. Freyja would always love her brother, but this was the first time she felt an overwhelming urge to protect him. It occurred to her that this must be how Frey felt every time she had an accident or was picked on.

"Thank you for the offer," he said. "But after being in bed for so long, I need to learn to walk all over again."

Away from the festival bonfires, Freyja could see the stars, and the moons looked so close she felt she could reach out and touch them. Frey asked her many questions as they trundled up the path. She recounted the Terracotta Forest, the gypsies with their caravans and patchwork tents, and the dwarves with their Astarite dragon forge in the mountain. When they reached the crest of the hill, Frey made an interesting observation. "It doesn't sound like Folke helped you at all."

"The night I went with him to heal the other children, I asked about that," she said, falling backwards on the blanket of snow and gazing up at the constellations. "In typical fashion he didn't answer me directly. Instead, he posed a question about whether I noticed that it didn't snow in the Terracotta forest."

"They do say the place is magical," said Frey, lying down next to her. "I think your new pet is testimony to that."

"Don't let Hemming hear you say that, he'll peck your eyes out." The falcon was resting back in her room, and she chuckled at the thought of his indignation at being referred to as a pet. "There is something about that forest because the trees always had golden leaves, and the meadow where we rested was full of grass and flowers like winter could not penetrate that place."

"And don't forget the walking undead. Strong spells are required to call upon them."

Freyja shuddered. "When I told Folke I did notice, he said that even though the forest may appear unchanging, it still is even if it's only in increments. He said we all change, sometimes quickly, sometimes slowly but it is inevitable. When he realised I had made the decision to find the brisingr stone, he said he wanted me to take responsibility of it. To own my actions and see it through."

"Then why accompany you at all? To observe?"

"I'm not sure. Maybe curiosity. I think he's always been interested in transformations and growth. The inside of his cottage is a jungle. I guess he saw something in me."

Frey looked sideways at his sister. "I've always seen it."

She reached out and took his gloved hand. "I was going to lose you. I needed to try." She sighed, a cloud of steam escaping from her mouth into the night. "I also asked Folke about my necklace and its powers."

"What did he say?"

"The necklace was forged using remnants of the Astarite star by the dwarves, so it always contained magic. Specifically, the potential for magic, he said. Somehow I unlocked it through my tears." Freyja paused in thought, her eyes reflecting the celestial bodies of Asmund and Asta absorbed into each other. "When I was prisoner in the storeroom, there was naught but dirt and dust. However, it was where the dwarves kept brisingr stones before. Folke believes I may have absorbed some of the brisingr dust, perhaps by inhaling or through my skin. Mixed into my blood, it fought off the tetanarium. That's his theory."

Freyja pondered the Asgardian blood that ran through her veins and her acute sensitivity to magic around her. The goblin needle she purchased from Pan, the molten sorcery within the dwarven vault, and the Astarite star all permeated their own magical signature. She learned they were all different to her touch, sight, and even taste. The brisingr tears she released was evidence that she had undergone some sort of transformation.

"I think old man Folke knows more than he lets on," Frey mused, squeezing his sister's hand.

"Perhaps. He did tell me one thing though about brisingr stones. In Midgard, they call them amber. I've no idea why he shared that with me."

"Amber? What a funny name."

"Don't get me started. You should hear the names of the Midgard herbs he has in his garden."

The twins laughed as they moved their arms and legs and formed angels in the snow. They lay there treasuring the moment, and Freyja whispered her thanks up at the twin moons. When it got too cold, they made their way back to the village, holding hands. The music of the moon festival, and the orange glow of bonfires inviting them to return to the celebrations. Freyja looked forward to eating her mother's cinnamon and tinkleberry pie, her necklace making her glow like a little star floating down the hill.

Epilogue

Freyja tied her hair into a knot, laced up her leather boots, and then gathered her things: food, waterskin, rope, blanket, tent, flint, steel, lantern, magic compass, and needle. Frey handed her some additional items to squeeze into her pack while Hemming flew in a wide arc overhead and let out a loud screech. As she pinned her cloak around her neck, she could feel the Brisingamen under her linen shirt. The necklace felt cool against her skin.

Torsten appeared with bow and arrow in hand, his own pack on his back, ready to leave. Freyja smiled, remembering when the two of them set off on their quest to find a tiny amber stone a month ago. This time her brother was here. He was still a little too skinny for her liking. The knuckles on his hands protruding out in a way that still reminded her of the tetanarium, but his strength was back. He had his yew bow strapped across his chest and was testing the weight of his sword, swinging it in fluid arcs while the deer on his oblong shield flashed sunlight on his off arm. He looked capable, brave, and fearless. This was the brother she knew.

"Stop gawking at me like that," he said. "You've seen me training again. You need not fear that my sword arm will break like a twig."

Freyja looked away, shielding her thoughts. The scent of spring was in the air, the grass sprouts began to show themselves on the hill amongst the patches of leftover snow. Hints of promise lay everywhere. New delphiniums and blossoms displayed welcome colours amongst the white. The naked trees in the orchards now gave birth to new leaves. There was a distinct difference in the atmosphere compared to her previous journey. Her first steps outside the village with Torsten were filled with desperation and urgency. This time, the urgency was still there, but now she felt a greater sense of hope. With her twin brother by her side, a greater sense of purpose also accompanied that hope.

Another squawk from Hemming sounded as if to remind her not to dawdle. The three young adventurers looked at each other. Freyja felt they had all changed in different ways, but overall, they were stronger and closer. With a deep breath, inhaling the invisible energy of Asgard, she felt vitality pump in her heart. "Shall we?" she asked.

Torsten nodded and Frey grinned.

"Absolutely," replied Frey. "Let's go find father."

Here ends book one
"Freyja and the Brisingamen Necklace".

The adventures and growth of young Freyja
continue in book two
"Freyja and the Falcon Cloak".

Manufactured by Amazon.ca
Bolton, ON